"Are you asking if I'm on the take?"
He turned then, and his eyes seemed sad.
"What do you think?"

She was stunned. "What should I think? You're my husband and I love you, but I've heard some pretty awful things about you lately."

He came and sat on the bed, reaching across to take her hand. "I guess it all boils down to trust, doesn't it?" he said quietly. "Either you trust me or you don't."

His mouth came down on hers, hard and demanding, but almost pleading, too. She responded to him fully, letting her passions flow in a desperate attempt to erase the memories of those accusations from her mind. Jake was her husband, the man she loved. She would have faith in him.

Adrienne Edwards *is a husband-and-wife writing team. After developing romance outlines together, they go to their separate word processors and work on different scenes; then they edit each other's writing. They reside with their four children, two dogs, and three cats in northeastern Illinois, and each coaches a children's soccer team in the spring and fall.*

Dear Reader:

One of the most exciting things about creating TO HAVE AND TO HOLD has been watching it emerge from the glimmer of an idea, into a firm concept, and finally into a line of books that is attracting an ever-increasing and loyal readership. TO HAVE AND TO HOLD is now ten months old, and that thrilling growth continues every month as we work with more and more talented writers, find brand new story ideas, and receive your thoughts and comments on the books.

More than ever, we are publishing books that offer all the elements you love in a romance—as well as the freshness and variety you crave. When you finish a TO HAVE AND TO HOLD book, we trust you'll experience the special glow of satisfaction that comes from reading a really good romance with a brand new twist.

And if any of your friends still question whether married love can be as compelling, heart-warming, and just plain fun as courtship, we hope you'll share your latest TO HAVE AND TO HOLD romance with them and dispel their doubts once and for all!

Best wishes for a fabulous summer,

Ellen Edwards

Ellen Edwards, Senior Editor
TO HAVE AND TO HOLD
The Berkley Publishing Group
200 Madison Avenue
New York, N.Y. 10016

P.S. Do you receive our SECOND CHANCE AT LOVE and TO HAVE AND TO HOLD newsletter? If not, be sure to fill out the coupon in the back of this book, and we'll send you the newsletter free of charge four times a year.

To Have and to Hold

HONORABLE INTENTIONS

ADRIENNE EDWARDS

SECOND CHANCE AT LOVE BOOK

HONORABLE INTENTIONS

Copyright © 1984 by Adrienne Edwards

All rights reserved. No part of this publication may be reproduced or transmitted in any form or by any means, electronic or mechanical, including photocopy, recording, or any information storage and retrieval system, without permission in writing from the publisher.

Requests for permission to make copies of any part of the work should be mailed to: Permissions, To Have and to Hold, The Berkley Publishing Group, 200 Madison Avenue, New York, NY 10016.

First edition published July 1984

First printing

"Second Chance at Love," the butterfly emblem, and "To Have and to Hold" are trademarks belonging to Jove Publications, Inc.

Printed in the United States of America

To Have and to Hold books are published by
The Berkley Publishing Group
200 Madison Avenue, New York, NY 10016

1

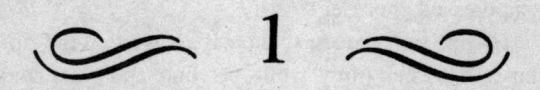

KAYE CORRIGAN PUT down her hair dryer and quickly ran a brush through her honey-colored hair. She hated being late, but there wasn't much she could do about it tonight. Not with that meeting of department managers at the store running so long, and Jake returning from court even later. She'd better resign herself to the inevitable. They would not get to the party on time.

She took out an array of makeup and began applying some base. Her skin was smooth and creamy, more like that of a teenager than a woman of twenty-nine, especially with that faint sprinkling of freckles over her nose. She thought she looked more sophisticated with the freckles covered by liquid makeup, even if Jake thought they were cute. After adding a little blusher to her high cheekbones and a touch of emerald shadow to enhance her green eyes, she was about to apply some mascara to her long, velvety lashes when she realized that the apartment was suspiciously quiet. Turning around, she glanced into the master bedroom. A black cat blinked at her from its perch on the corner of the dresser, but Jake was not in sight.

"Are you ready, Jake? We don't have much time."

"I'm always ready," his deep voice responded with a suppressed chuckle.

Her lips tightened suspiciously, Kaye tied the ribbon-sash of her filmy white peignoir and went into the bedroom. There on the bed was Jake, his back against the headboard and his well-muscled legs stretched out across the quilted bedspread. His attire consisted of a towel.

"I thought you said you were ready. You don't have a stitch of clothing on."

"Clothes and ready are mutually exclusive."

Kaye willed herself to stay in the doorway, ignoring both Jake's obvious invitation and the warm glow spreading through her body. Her gaze traveled along his muscular arms and over the hairy chest that tapered slightly to his narrow waist. Her senses were reminding her wildly how she liked his roughness against her own smooth skin, but she forced herself to be stern.

"This is my boss's party, remember? We can't afford to get Matt irritated if I ever hope to be more than just the manager of the lingerie department."

"Sure, we can." His voice was silky and persuasive. "Timmerman's Department Store can fire you if they want to. I could support you if you'd let me."

She laughed. "Don't forget I know what judges make, and the only thing you're earning is respect."

"I have some hidden assets," he noted and shifted his body so that the towel fell away.

"And some not so hidden."

Jake smiled invitingly from where he lay, and her eyes lingered on his mobile lips. She could almost feel them on her body, kissing, caressing, tasting. She grew warm at the thought.

"Why don't you come over here so we can discuss this in greater detail?" he asked.

"What's to discuss?"

"True, talking's unnecessary. We'll go straight to action."

"Jake." She laughed in spite of herself. "We're due at the party, remember?"

"No one will notice if we're not there."

Kaye tried to look stern, but failed miserably. How could she resist the temptation of that sensuous mouth? Or the gentle, knowing touch of Jake's strong hands? She'd much rather be lying there next to him, letting his caress persuade her to stay. The trouble was that she'd rather spend the whole evening that way, and not just the next half-hour. If only the two of them could relax over a simple dinner, then love the hours away without any thought for the time or anyone else. But she had assured Matt less than an hour ago that they'd be at his party. And since one of the reasons he was giving it was to celebrate her nomination to the presidency of the local merchants' association, Kaye felt it would be distinctly rude not to put in an appearance.

She made one last attempt to get him out of bed. "John Wilson Corrigan, if you don't get dressed right now, I'll never speak to you again."

With a devilish gleam in his blue eyes, he slid down and stretched out on the bed. "Make me."

Kaye's mind told her to get back in the dressing room, but her body propelled her onto the bed. Her tall, slender frame straddled Jake's husky one as she settled herself into a comfortable position on his stomach. They were going to be late anyway, so why not give in to her desires? Being a little later wouldn't matter. Her hands slid over Jake's chest and found his armpits. Her fingers wiggled slightly.

"Hey, that's not what I had in mind," he protested. His sleepy, sensuous look was gone. "Behave yourself."

He tried to grab her wrists to stop her from tickling, but she snatched them away. Then she leaned back, sliding her hands down his bent legs to the soles of his feet, where she knew he was even more ticklish.

"Kaye, stop that," Jake ordered.

When he moved his feet away from her, she simply reached for the sensitive spot behind his knees. "I've never met a man as ticklish as you are," she said with a smile.

"Oh?" He made another unsuccessful dive for her hands. "And how many have you tested?"

"Hundreds. Maybe even thousands."

"You've had it now, lady." His eyes gleamed with

Honorable Intentions

mischief as he heaved his shoulders up. The force of the movement made her lose her balance, and she fell onto the bed. He rolled on top of her, grabbing her hands with one of his and pinning them above her head.

"Come on, Jake. It was just a joke."

"Go on, plead some more. We judges enjoy hearing people plead."

His free hand reached between their bodies to untie the sash of her peignoir and push it out of the way. Then the hand deftly removed her negligee and slid along her side, not quite tickling, but not quite pleasuring either.

"Jake, be nice," she coaxed.

He grinned wickedly and leaned down to kiss her ear. His tongue darted inside quickly, but before she could enjoy the sensation, his hand tickled her, and she tried in vain to twist away from him.

Pleading would do no good, so she began to fight back in her own way. She maneuvered one of her legs between his and, as Jake teased her, she rubbed it against him, stirring him a way that she knew only she could. The tips of her breasts brushed against his hairy chest and stirred up longings in her that increased the fervor of her movements. Her hunger for him grew.

Jake forgot about his desire for revenge as his body demanded fulfillment. His teasing hands began to soothe and stroke, building in Kaye an intense desire that seemed ready to burst. Nothing else seemed real or necessary to her but the feel of his skin against hers, the touch of his caress.

His lips sought hers, rough and fierce as they tasted and devoured. The moist recesses of his mouth seemed to drain the life from her body and put it back again, renewed and stronger, but dependent on him for life. His tongue began to explore her mouth, its turgid fullness creating still new desires as her body throbbed to his pulse.

Then, suddenly, his lips were on her neck, urging that pulsating point to further and greater limits. Her blood was racing, fiery and demanding, as it rushed to the point of contact with him, her source of life, her source of love. His kisses trailed onto her shoulder and her breasts until her skin was afire with the urgency of his need.

"Do you know how the thought of you ties me up in knots all day?" he murmured. His hand moved between her legs, finding the core of her womanhood. It seemed to leap beneath his touch, sending waves of longing through her.

"It's not so easy for me to forget you, either." Her voice was little more than a breathless whisper, the reflection of her body's desperate cravings for him. He was her lover, her friend, her knight in shining armor.

"I hope not."

Unable to wait any longer, Kaye moved her legs under him, and Jake entered her lovingly. Her eyes closed, she clung to him, moving in an ageless rhythm that sent her soaring through time and space. He was the only reality in her rapidly fading universe. He alone mattered to her.

"I love you." His voice was hoarse and beautiful,

the words whispered as they were totally one in body and in spirit.

She floated back to earth entangled in his arms. Side by side, they clung together as their breathing slowed and their blood ceased to race. Their lovemaking was as powerfully exciting as it had been when they were first married seven and a half months ago. Just touching each other drove them wild with need and longing.

Kaye felt a nuzzling on her neck and opened her eyes. "We still have a party to go to," she reminded Jake.

"Where have you been? We're having our own party. In fact, I've even got a present for you." He got up from the bed. "Close your eyes."

"Wasn't that a present you just gave me?" Kaye joked, but did as he asked. "We really do have to go to Matt's party, you—"

She stopped as something light and cool touched the skin around her neck. Her hands flew up to feel the chain and some sort of pendant.

"Happy anniversary," Jake whispered. His lips caressed the back of her neck, making her body tingle with renewed desire.

Kaye bent her head, looking down to see the pear-shaped diamond on a gold chain hanging between her breasts. She fingered it wonderingly. "Oh, Jake, it's gorgeous, but it's not our anniversary."

"Sure it is," he said. "We've been married exactly seven months and two weeks."

"You're an idiot," she said, turning toward him. "But I love you."

She put her arms around his neck and pressed her body against his. The flame of their passion ignited once more, and his arms closed around her. She kissed his lips and his neck, pink and tender from recent shaving, then laid her head against his chest. He was so wonderful to her. She had never met anyone quite like her Jake, considerate and loving and always a man she could respect.

"You know, I don't need things like this. You do a very good job of expressing your love in other ways—ways that won't put us in hock for the rest of our lives."

"Actually, it's a bribe," he said. His hands slid over her bare back. "I was hoping you'd be so overwhelmed that you'd want to stay home tonight and show me how grateful you are."

She pushed away from him with a smile. "Are you kidding? Now we have to go so I can show this off."

"Swell."

She just laughed and stood up. "Jake."

"I know, I know. Get dressed. Boy, this had better be one terrific party."

Matt's house was about a half-hour's drive from their home on the north side of Chicago, and Kaye enjoyed the ride even though she knew they were late. The air was cool and crisp, just the way late October was supposed to be in the upper Midwest. And once they were out in the suburbs near Matt's home, the night sky was filled with stars.

"It sure is lovely out here," Kaye sighed. "Imagine

taking long walks and watching the leaves change color."

"There speaks someone who never raked a leaf in her life."

That was true, she had to admit. She had always lived in apartments, but then neither was Jake the overworked raker he made himself out to be. She'd seen the house he grew up in, with its tiny yard and solitary tree.

"I thought you liked the apartment," Jake said, interrupting her thoughts. "What's the matter? You suddenly want leaves to rake and sidewalks to shovel?"

"No, not really. I loved your apartment from the moment I saw it, and we wouldn't find anything as convenient to our jobs. But as a kid I always thought it would be great to have my own yard, and every once in a while the idea returns."

He stopped at a traffic light and turned toward her, squeezing her hand fondly. "No reason why we couldn't buy a house, if that's what you want. We could sell the three-flat or just sublet our present apartment with the other two."

"Now is not the time to buy a house. Have you noticed the interest rates lately?"

The light changed, and he let go of her hand as he drove ahead. "Are you kidding? A housing court judge can name his own rate of interest," he teased.

"Jake, be serious. I am not interested in moving."

They parked the car and walked to a large Queen Anne–style house, brightly lit by outside lights. Even though it was night, the intricate carpentry work on the trim of the house was noticeable.

"This place must have cost a good bit of change," Jake muttered as she rang the doorbell. "Is it the type of house you want?"

"I told you, I don't want to move. Can't you drop the subject, or do I have to get tough?"

"Is that as in whips and chains and bondage?" he teased.

She punched him playfully. "I thought that as you got older you thought about sex less."

"That's true. Since I'm a venerable thirty-eight now, I should only think about it every eight seconds. However, I'm still on the newlywed rate of once every three seconds."

"You're impossible."

"Insatiable is the word," he corrected.

The door before them swung open, and a balding man in his fifties greeted them enthusiastically. "Kaye, I missed you. Judy and I were afraid you weren't going to make it. And how could we party without our presidential candidate?" He reached forward to shake Jake's hand. "Good evening, Judge. It's nice of you to come."

Jake nodded. "Glad to," he replied.

"Jake got an important call just before we were set to leave," Kaye said, leaning forward for Matt's kiss on her cheek. She ignored Jake's muffled snort. "Sorry we're late."

Matt stepped aside to let them in and then took their coats.

"Why didn't you tell him that the call was from

my wife, who wanted her voracious sexual appetite satisfied?"

"Would you behave?" she hissed. Then her expression cleared as Matt returned to lead them into the living room.

"Just make yourselves at home," he said. "I think you know everybody. Call out if you want something you can't find."

"Want to ask him where his whips are?" Jake whispered.

She sighed in exasperation, thankful that Matt had moved away toward some of the other guests. "Will you get me some white wine, please? And stay out of trouble."

Kaye watched fondly as Jake moved through the crowd to the bar. He stopped to chat with several people and smiled across the room at a few others. He had such presence, such charisma, that he naturally attracted people. In fact, she was rather amazed and proud that he had chosen to marry her. The way women flocked around him, he could have had his pick of the eligible females in the city. She smiled at him when he returned with her wine.

"Didn't you get anything for yourself, hon?"

"No, I'm not thirsty." He leaned forward and whispered, "Besides no wine can compete with the taste of your kisses."

A warm glow spread through Kaye that was not due to the alcohol she had sipped. "Keep it up and you may not get any chance to sleep tonight."

"We could just leave now," he suggested.

Kaye squeezed his arm, but shook her head. "Look, there's Ned Schatzen. I didn't know any of your political buddies were going to be here."

"Who said he's my buddy?"

To Kaye's astonishment, Jake sounded edgy. She shrugged and tried to explain. "Well, he is a real-estate lawyer and you're a housing court judge. I only meant he was someone you knew."

"You're right. I'm just being ornery tonight." He reached over and took a sip of her wine. "I guess that's what happens when you marry a luscious young woman. You'd rather stay at her side than have a drink with the boys. Can you spare me for a few minutes while I say hello?"

"I'll try."

Kaye's eyes followed Jake as he joined Ned and another man. Although Jake laughed and talked easily enough, he somehow didn't seem himself. He was standing stiffly, as he did when he was tense or over exhausted.

Maybe they should have stayed home. They both had worked long hours this week and she knew he was tired. She'd keep an eye on the time and see that they left early.

Kaye walked through the crowd, stopping to talk now and then. Most of the people she knew were fellow department managers from Timmerman's, but a few of her artistic friends from the city's north side were there, too. Newspaper and television reporters, two dancers from an experimental dance troupe, and a couple of professors from State University.

"Congratulations, Kaye."

She turned to find a young boutique owner at her side.

"I just heard today that you've been nominated to the presidency of the Greater Avenue Merchants' Association for next year. Hope you big store people won't forget us little retailers."

Kaye laughed. "No chance of that, Denise. The big stores and little stores need each other. In fact, once the city acquires that old abandoned factory building on Crawford, I'd like to see it turned into a specialty mall."

"Great. Maybe Jake can speed things up for you." Denise flashed her a smile, then drifted off on the arm of a man who did carpeting commercials on local television.

After several hours of conversation, two more glasses of white wine, and a sampling of various hors d'oeuvres, Kaye went in search of Jake. She thought they could safely leave now without hurting anyone's feelings.

She found him standing in a corner of Matt's basement rec room. There was a pool game going on nearby, but Jake was still deep in conversation with Ned and another man. Kaye slipped up behind her husband and put her arm through his. He paused to smile down at her. The love shining in his eyes made her knees weaken and her heart race.

"Ready to go?" he asked.

She nodded.

"Just give me five minutes for a quick trip to the bathroom." He said his good-byes and put his arm around her shoulders. Together they went back upstairs. "How about if I meet you at the door?"

While Jake headed toward the bathroom at the back of the house, Kaye went off in search of their coats, which she found lying across a bed in an upstairs room. She picked them up as two other women entered the room.

"Kaye, how marvelous to see you here. I noticed that Jake spent the evening talking to Ned. What a shame we didn't have any time to chat ourselves."

Kaye smiled politely at Carol Schatzen. An evening with Carol was not her idea of a good time, but marriage to Jake had made her more politically astute and diplomatic. "Yes, it is. But maybe we can get together some time soon."

"That would be wonderful." Carol turned toward the younger woman who had come in with her. "I don't think you've met Maggie Kann. Her husband is an associate in Ned's firm—he was talking to Jake tonight with Ned."

"Pleased to meet you." Kaye reached forward to take Maggie's extended hand.

"It's nice meeting you," Maggie murmured.

"Actually, Maggie and I have just become neighbors," Carol went on. "She and her Bill bought a lovely three-acre plot only a mile or so from us."

"I'll bet you have a lot of leaves to rake."

The other two women laughed. "Are you still living in that converted brownstone on the north side?" Carol asked. "We bought a building in that area a few months ago that should really turn us a nice profit if we can manage the city inspectors. Think Jake could keep them off our backs?"

Honorable Intentions   15

Kaye frowned. Surely Carol couldn't be casting a slur on Jake's integrity? "Off your backs? I really don't see how Jake could do anything... I mean, he's a *judge*..."

"Exactly," Carol purred. She and Maggie exchanged amused glances, and Kaye felt her irritation grow. Clearly Carol hadn't understood her delicate way of saying that her husband wouldn't do anything illegal. Coolly, she told the two women, "If you two will excuse me, Jake is waiting for me downstairs."

Carol put her hand on Kaye's arm. "Kaye, don't get huffy. You can trust us, but I'll have Ned ask Jake himself. I'm sure they'll be able to work something out. We'll leave the men to do the work while we enjoy the benefits, eh?"

Kaye was no longer irritated; she was angry. "Why is it I get the feeling you're talking about something underhanded? I don't know what Ned might be involved in, but I assure you Jake is very, very scrupulous."

Carol pulled back. Her eyes grew hard, and her voice was mocking. "Oh, my. Aren't we the outraged innocent? Tell us how you two are just barely scraping by. Tuna fish for dinner three times a week and clothes bought at a resale shop. Or tell us how Jake managed, on his thirty-five thousand a year, to pay full market value for that building you live in."

"He bought it several years ago, with money he had saved when he was in private practice." Kaye knew she didn't have to make any explanations, but she was too angry to be silent. "He did *not* buy it with kickbacks, as you seem to be suggesting, or use his office to lower the price."

"He saved all of his pennies in a piggy bank, right? The perfect boy scout: thrifty, honest, and true." Maggie giggled quietly as Carol went on, "Maybe you'd better have a talk with Jake and see how clean you are before you play holier than thou again."

"Just because we aren't pinching pennies doesn't mean that Jake is involved in anything illegal," Kaye protested, struggling to keep her composure. "We both earn good salaries and can afford a few luxuries, but we certainly don't have the money to run out and buy everything we want."

She pushed past the two women, clutching the coats to her as if they could control her angry trembling. Carol didn't try to stop her this time, but her voice broke the stillness just as Kaye reached the door.

"Oh, Kaye darling, I almost forgot to mention how I love your necklace. Was it a gift from Jake? It must be wonderful to have such a generous husband."

Jake glanced over at Kaye. They were halfway home from the party and she still hadn't said a word. That wasn't like her. He wondered if something was wrong, but it was hard to tell with Kaye. Maybe she just was in a quiet mood, or maybe she was tired. He thought he was getting pretty good at reading her moods, but seven and half months of marriage wasn't a very long time. He still wasn't always sure when to push and when to leave her alone.

He turned onto River Drive and drove another mile or so. The silence was getting to him. Relaxed, sleepy

Honorable Intentions 17

silence he could take, but there seemed to be a lot of tension in the air.

"You sure are chatty tonight."

She shrugged in reply.

"Tired?"

"I guess."

"How about a Corrigan's super-special head-to-toe massage when we get home?"

"That would be nice," she replied. But in the glow from the stoplight, her smile looked forced to him.

She turned back to gazing out her window, and Jake concentrated on his driving. In a few uncomfortable minutes they were home, but the silence continued after they parked the car and went inside. Kaye did bend down and play quietly with Nip and Tuck, their two cats, and her voice was quiet and soothing. Jake couldn't hear any hint of anger in it. So she *had* merely been tired.

But as he watched her scratch the cats for a few minutes, he felt strangely out of place. The cats were ignoring him, and apparently so was Kaye. He went into the bedroom and undressed, putting on his robe and lying down on top of the bed as he waited for her. She came in a short while later. It might have been his imagination, but her eyes seemed to be avoiding him.

"Need any help with the necklace?" he offered.

"No." She opened her jewelry box. "I took it off already."

She went into the dressing room and came out a few minutes later in a long-sleeved cotton nightshirt.

It was what she normally wore when she had menstrual cramps and wasn't feeling very sexy. Maybe that explained it, Jake thought.

"Your period start?"

"No, it's due next week. I just felt a little cold."

"Oh." He was not sure an offer to warm her up would be appreciated, especially when she walked past the bed to sit in the armchair, so he said nothing further.

"Did you have a good time tonight?" she asked. Her voice was quiet and tentative. Why? he wondered.

"It was fine."

"At least you had Ned and Bill to talk to, so you weren't bored."

He would have been much happier if they hadn't been there. For once, he'd wanted to relax and be himself. "I wouldn't have been bored without them. I like your friends."

She nodded. "I know, but I was still glad some of your friends were there."

"Just because I work with them doesn't mean they're my friends," he snapped.

"No, it doesn't," Kaye agreed.

Jake took a deep breath. He hadn't meant for that sharpness to creep into his voice, but there were times when everything got to be too much. He wished he could pour out the whole story to her, but that wasn't allowed.

"I have to deal with all kinds of people, Kaye. Some of them I like; others I have to tolerate. Anyway"—he patted the bed next to him—"come over here so I can warm you up."

Honorable Intentions 19

She seemed to hesitate, then walked slowly over to the bed, but instead of lying down and snuggling up to him as she usually did, she put her pillow up against the headboard and sat back against it. She pulled her knees up and hugged them to her chest as she stared at the far wall.

After a moment, she spoke again. "You know, Jake, we have a lot of loose ends."

"Loose ends?" he asked.

"Well, we don't have a will."

He looked at her, but did not reply.

"I thought you lawyers were always pushing for things like that. Doesn't the bar association run public service announcements on the horrors of not having a will?"

"Why this sudden interest in our financial affairs?" he asked guardedly.

She didn't reply immediately, continuing to look away. "The end of the year is coming, and I assume that we're going to file a joint return."

"I'm assuming that also," Jake said evenly.

"Well, we really don't know the details of each other's finances."

"My salary is a matter of public record."

"But do you have any other income?"

"Just from the investments I made while I was in private practice. You know that."

"But there seems to be quite a bit of it."

"So I made some successful investments." He could show her the stock certificates. He wasn't trying to hide them. "Occasionally, even judges get lucky. Why all the questions suddenly?"

She shrugged, but didn't exactly answer him. "I know our mortgage payments are low, but I'm not sure that we can afford this building on your salary alone. What if we decided to have a baby and I stopped working for a while? Could we still live here or would we have to move?"

He wished this sudden interest had been caused by a desire to start a family, if for no other reason than that it was preferable to the other possibilities running through his head. But he knew maternal instincts had nothing to do with this conversation, someone had said something about him to Kaye at that damn party. If only he could approach the whole subject openly! But that was impossible—he couldn't tell Kaye the truth, and he didn't want to lie to her.

"Yes, we could stay here," he admitted.

Now it was Kaye's turn to be quiet. "You know, Jake, I do have a business degree with a concentration in finance. I'm not stupid, and I would like to get more involved in our family finances."

He didn't know what to say, didn't know what he could say.

"I thought that married couples were supposed to share things," she said.

Not everything. There were some things he wasn't allowed to share. Not even with his wife. That had been made very clear to him when he decided to marry her. He had been ordered to keep her in the dark, and he had agreed. Of course, he had thought it wouldn't be for very long, maybe a month at most, for things had seemed to be wrapping up. But he had guessed wrong and then had lived with the hope that she

Honorable Intentions

wouldn't hear rumors. It seemed his luck had run out.

He pulled off his robe and threw it on a chair close by. Then he got under the covers, lying on his side so that he looked away from her.

"Jake, were you listening to me?"

"We'll go through it."

"When?"

"Soon, honey. Real soon."

He felt her getting off the bed. "I'm not too sleepy now, Jake. I think I'll read for a while."

"Okay, good night." He tried to sound casual.

"Good night, Jake." She left the room.

He had been a fool to think she wouldn't hear anything. How had he ever thought he could keep it quiet? Rumors abounded. He should have known that some would get back to her.

It was just that he had loved her so, right from the beginning, and when she returned his love, nothing else seemed to matter. Besides, he told himself, everything would be over before she ever learned about it, so there was no need to make any explanations.

Now she was doubting him, and she had every reason to. Could he stall her for a while, or would that only make more trouble? How could he keep her trust when appearances looked so damning?

2

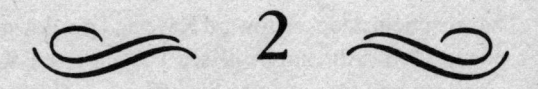

KAYE PAGED LISTLESSLY through an old copy of *Life* magazine, then threw it onto a pile of other magazines and stared across the office. The dark-paneled walls spoke of long-standing respectability and contrasted sharply with the starkly modern lobby downstairs. Jones and Abrahms was a relatively new law firm, but when the partners had set up their offices about ten years ago, they had bought the paneling from an old, run-down building and had it transplanted here. Instant age and wisdom.

She got to her feet. Few things were what they seemed to be these days. Wasn't that why she was here? To prove to herself that Jake was not dishonest, no matter how things might look.

And she admitted to herself that they didn't look very good. Even though she wanted to believe the best of Jake, all sorts of things kept coming back to her with new and sinister meanings. The money he had spent on her during their engagement and first few months of marriage. Jokes about bribery and seemingly innocent remarks about money. The necklace. Everything seemed to point to Jake's guilt, but she still couldn't believe he was dishonest. Not her Jake. Those women at the party were just troublemakers.

The receptionist looked toward Kaye and put down her phone. "Mr. Abrahms will see you now, miss. His secretary will show you to his office.

Kaye stood up, wishing she could bolt instead. She could not believe that she was doing this. Using a false name and asking some unknown lawyer about Jake. If Jake ever found out, it would look as if she hadn't trusted him. And a marriage without trust was nothing. She should leave now.

But her feet stayed riveted to the spot. Jake hadn't done anything wrong, and she was only going to confirm his innocence. That way she would be able to relax once and for all. She didn't want the rest of her life to be as confused as the past weekend. She had hated feeling so uncertain.

A gray-haired woman approached her. "Would you come with me, Miss Sanders?"

Being addressed by her maiden name made her feel worse, as if she had already found Jake guilty and was ashamed to share his name. She followed the woman down the hall wondering if it was too late to change her mind. She found herself entering an office.

A tall, thin man got up from the desk. "Hello, Miss Sanders. Won't you have a seat?"

As she acknowledged his greeting, the palms of her hands were suddenly wet with nervous persperation. Wasn't her very presence here jeopardizing her marriage?

The lawyer's eyes were on her, and she forced herself to recite the lines she had rehearsed. "I...I have some interest in our family trust. And we have some properties in the city that may wind up in housing court. I was wondering what kind of man the judge—I think his name is Corrigan—is."

She felt sick, certain that Mr. Abrahms knew who she really was and was planning at the moment how he would tell Jake. But he just looked at her quietly.

"Actually, I don't deal in real-estate and property matters," he said. "But I have heard about Judge Corrigan. Everybody has."

"Everybody?" Her heart caught in fear.

"Everybody in law circles, I mean."

"Oh." Jake was a judge, she told herself. Of course, lawyers would have heard of him.

They were both silent for a moment, and then Mr. Abrahms went on. "Our society doesn't value civil servants very highly. This is especially true for judges. If the judge is a good attorney, as he should be, he can make anywhere from five to ten times as much in private practice."

Kaye blinked in surprise.

"And this causes many good men to leave the judiciary or avoid it altogether. Those who stay tend to supplement their income."

Kaye's jaw tightened. "Supplement?"

"Free lunches. Discounts from local merchants. Country club privileges extended by corporations. Many of these supplements can't really be called bribes. Nothing is asked for and nothing is given. People do it just to create an atmosphere of conviviality. But there are those who request specific sums for specific actions. These are very definitely bribes."

"And Judge Corrigan?"

"One of the most corrupt judges, I'm afraid."

She bit her lip and gulped back the sudden churning of her stomach.

"He had an older brother, Bill, who was also a judge, and always seemed open to persuasion, if you get my meaning."

She nodded stiffly, realizing how little she knew about Bill, other than that he had died in an automobile accident a few years ago. Jake was still so upset by his brother's death that he rarely mentioned him.

Mr. Abrahms continued, "Apparently, John Corrigan is following in his brother's footsteps—only more so. He very openly is willing to sell anything, including his mother's virtue, for a price."

The words made her feel sick to her stomach. No, that wasn't Jake. Not her Jake. She could feel tears welling up in her eyes. She had to get out of here before she heard any more. Lies, a misunderstanding... Perhaps this lawyer had some kind of animus against Jake. There had to be some explanation...

Honorable Intentions

Mr. Abrahms smiled at her. "Does that help in any way?"

Help? How could hearing him malign her husband help anything? "Yes, yes," she stammered, trying to remember the role she was playing. "I think I know what to do now." She rose to her feet.

The lawyer stood up also. "Would you like one of my associates to handle Judge Corrigan for you? Ted Martin is very capable and has had plenty of experience in housing court."

"I need to think about it," she said vaguely. "I'll get back to you, shall I?"

Without waiting for an answer, she fled down the hall. Luckily, she remembered seeing a ladies' room across from the elevators and took refuge there. Tears streamed down her cheeks, and her legs seemed barely able to support her. She sank into the single chair there, thankful that the room was empty.

What should she do now? Confront Jake openly? But that was tantamount to accusing him, and despite everything, she still couldn't believe Jake guilty of any wrongdoing. Instinctively, she felt he was honest. And yet she wished she had never gone to see Mr. Abrahms, that they had never gone to that party Friday night.

Jake took a drink of his ice water and glanced blindly around the bar. He was so tired of the lies and deception, and sick with worry about what was happening to Kaye. Even knowing the truth, there were days when he felt dirty and tainted. How must she feel? He just wished there was something he could say to make it all right, to convince her to trust him. If only they could go back to the beginning. They had been so happy then, and interested only in each other.

Actually, they had met in this very restaurant. It had been last December, during the usual crowded lunch hour...

"Sorry, Judge," Hans had told him. "But it'll be almost an hour's wait."

Jake had frowned in thought. His calendar wasn't busy for that afternoon. Maybe he should just take a walk and come back later. He was turning to go when he saw her: the loveliest woman imaginable, and sitting alone at a table for two.

Her hair was the color of honey and lay in soft curls on her shoulders. She was slender, with an air of grace about her. The way she held her wine glass, even the way she sat, bespoke elegance... and a sensuality that the dark gray business suit she wore couldn't disguise.

"Who is she?" he asked Hans.

But the waiter didn't know. "This is the first time I've seen her, but she's not wearing a wedding ring."

Jake grinned at the man. "Are you that observant of all your customers?"

"Just part of the job, Your Honor."

"Would it also be part of the job to know if she's waiting for anyone?"

Hans shook his head. "Party of one." He smiled slowly. "Of course, she might be willing to change that."

Jake slipped a bill from his wallet into Hans's hand. "Tell her I have an important court date this afternoon;

otherwise I wouldn't dream of imposing."

The waiter nodded and pocketed the money as he went through the tables to where the blonde sat. Jake watched as Hans spoke to her, looking earnest and slightly apologetic. The woman looked over at Jake. He put on his best judicial expression, hoping it was the right mixture of sincerity and power. She smiled, and the room lit up for him.

Without being aware of moving, Jake was suddenly at the table. She was even more beautiful close up. Vaguely, he heard Hans introducing him.

"How do you do, Your Honor," she said politely as she offered her hand. "I'm Kaye Sanders."

"I hope you don't mind my intrusion."

"Not at all," she said.

Jake ordered his usual lunch of ham hocks and sauerkraut, and Hans left. "Do you work downtown?" he asked.

"No, I just came down to see the Christmas decorations," she told him.

She had a low, melodic voice that he felt he could listen to forever.

"I work along North River Drive," she went on, "but I've always preferred the decorations in the old downtown area. My father always brought me here to see them, and then we would have lunch here at Otto's."

"And are they as good as they were other years?"

"I don't know," she admitted with a laugh. "I decided to break tradition and eat first."

She had asked him about his work, but he never could remember afterward what he had said. He just couldn't stop looking at her. Her mouth was moist and inviting, and he wanted to capture it with his. Her hands looked gentle but strong, and he imagined them touching his body, arousing his senses into a desperate passion. By the time the meal was over, he knew he could not let her out of his sight and invited himself along to see the Christmas decorations.

"But what about your court date?" she asked, clearly puzzled.

"I'll grant a continuance. It'll only take a minute."

She stared at him, uncertain whether he was joking or not.

"I fibbed," he admitted with a grin. "There's nothing on my docket for this afternoon."

"Are you really a judge or did you fib about that, too?"

"Oh, no. I'm a judge, all right. On my honor. Want to see me in my robes?"

She burst into laughter as they stood up. "Maybe," she said. "We'll see what kind of a job you do judging the decorations."

He had helped her into her coat and led her out of the restaurant. That afternoon had been so glorious, and during the ensuing courtship he had felt as if nothing could ever come between them...

"Hey, Judge." Hans's voice caused Jake to look up sharply. "I found this beautiful lady hanging around the entryway."

Kaye was standing next to the balding waiter. Her somber expression brought him quickly back to the present.

"I tried to tell her that I was available," the waiter went on. "But, no, she had to have a judge. Balding men of substance aren't in style anymore." He laughed as he patted his substantial girth.

Jake forced himself to appear in good spirits. "Don't worry about it, Hans. Life is a pendulum. You'll be back in fashion one of these days."

"I don't know, Judge." He shook his head. "This health-food fad is really hanging on. I've even had some regulars coming in here wanting to know if we serve bean sprouts."

Jake laughed and took heart from the fact that Kaye smiled a little as the waiter seated her. "What did you tell him?"

"I told him that sauerkraut was just German bean sprouts. You two want your usual glass of Moselle?"

"Yes, please," Jake replied.

As the waiter went away, Jake noticed that Kaye's expression was somber again. "Didn't you want a glass of wine? I'm sorry, I didn't think to ask. I'm sure Hans will take it back."

"No, no. That's all right. I could use a drink."

That awful silence returned. Jake wished he could reassure her and keep her from getting hurt, but he didn't know how. He wasn't even certain right now just what was bothering her. If he started confiding in her, he might find himself in real trouble. He could only wait—wait and hurt—until she was ready to talk about it, and then gauge his responses to what she said.

Jake opened his menu, more for something to do than from a need to study it. He already knew what he would order. He and Kaye had lunch together every Tuesday, rotating between this German restaurant, an Italian one, and a Chinese one. Here, he always had his customary ham hocks and sauerkraut while Kaye went through the menu. She said life needed variety.

The wine came, but Kaye seemed not to notice. She was still staring off into the far end of the room.

"Kaye, what's wrong?"

She looked up in surprise, her eyes blinking and finally focusing on the wineglass in front of her. She picked up the glass and sipped her wine without replying.

Hans came by, his pad and pencil out. "If you two want to sit around, you'd better order something. I don't get paid to watch lovebirds swooning over each other."

"Your charm is exceeded only by your waist size," Jake replied.

Hans addressed himself to Kaye. "The man's a real comic. When crooks go out of style, he'll have a profession to fall back on."

Kaye was not amused. "I'll have whatever he's having."

Hans nodded and left.

Jake drank some of his wine. "Mad at me about something?"

"Should I be?"

"That means yes. When are you going to clue me in on the reason?"

Kaye drank some of her wine. "Nothing's wrong. I'm just tired. I didn't sleep well last night."

He didn't ask why not, but made small talk until

their meal arrived. He gratefully concentrated on his, quickly cleaning his plate. Kaye just picked at hers.

Hans came by to take the plates. "If my mother saw this, you wouldn't leave the table until you finished," he chided Kaye.

"I guess I'm lucky that your mother isn't here," she replied with a tight smile.

He came back with a coffeepot. "We have your favorite today, Mrs. Corrigan. German chocolate cake. How about a thick slice with a little ice cream on it?"

"I'm really not too hungry, Hans. Thank you just the same." This time her smile looked wan, and her eyes close to tears.

Jake couldn't take it anymore. They had to get this out in the open. Of course, he couldn't be totally open with her, but at least he could ask for her trust...

"What do you say we go away over the weekend?" he suggested. "We can drive over to Galena and make it a little vacation. Leave Friday afternoon and come back Monday morning. It's not too far."

Kaye didn't reply.

"Come on, Kaye. It'll be good for us to get away. Like a second honeymoon."

She looked at him sadly, and he reached across the table to take her hand. "Kaye, I love you. You know that, don't you?"

She squeezed his hand in return. "Galena should be pretty this time of year."

Her voice was quiet, and she didn't smile, but it was a start.

3

AS JAKE TIPPED the bellman, Kaye stared out the hotel window without really seeing the late fall landscape. She had always liked the stark beauty of this rolling hill country in northwestern Illinois, but she wasn't in the mood to appreciate it today.

"Well, lazybones, what do you want to do?" Jake came over to her looking full of energy. "Hiking, horseback riding, or a little bedroom wrestling?"

Normally, at the end of that kind of question he would have rolled her onto the bed, and the two of them would have tussled like two bear cubs, laughing and teasing each other until they were exhausted. But today Jake sounded tentative. The bright smile on his face didn't reach his eyes. Kaye knew he was reflecting her mood, but she didn't know what to do about it.

When she didn't answer, Jake gently put an arm around her hips and drew her to him. He sat down with Kaye on his lap, lightly kissing her on the cheek. His tenderness brought her close to tears. "So what's our plan for the afternoon?"

"I don't know," she said, continuing to stare out the window. "Do you have anything special that you'd like to do?"

Habit made her expect a leer followed by a rough hug and kiss, but Jake was still for a moment. Then he gently turned her face toward him. He kissed her lightly on the lips and looked soberly into her eyes.

"The only thing I'd really like to do is make you happy," he said. "And I don't seem to be doing that very well lately."

A quiver of her lips reminded her of her uneasy self-control, and she slid off his lap. "Excuse me a minute."

She managed to close the bathroom door before the first tear escaped. Leaning against the sink, she felt the tear slowly make a path down her cheek and onto the side of her jaw.

She loved Jake. She never doubted that, but did she really know him? From their first meeting, they'd been swept into a whirlwind of passion and excitement. When they had married a few months later, she was certain he was the best and dearest man she had ever met.

Jake was kind and thoughtful, forever putting her wishes ahead of his own. He always insisted they see

Honorable Intentions 37

the movie *she* wanted to see or eat at the kind of restaurant *she* wanted to eat at. He still bought her presents for no special occasion. Little things like flowers and candy, or bigger things like the necklace or this weekend away.

He hated to see her upset, even if she was just crying over a sad movie. He would tease and cajole her, not happy himself until she was laughing again.

He had never gotten along with her mother since she openly admitted she didn't like politicians, but when her mother was hospitalized last summer, he had rearranged his schedule so that they could fly out to California. He had stayed at Kaye's side the whole time only because he cared about her and knew that she needed him.

And what about the time she had that terrible cold and couldn't go to a political fund-raiser with him? He had tried to call her in the middle of the dinner, not knowing their phone was out of order. When he couldn't reach her, he raced home, terrified something had happened. And brought the police along.

What in the world was wrong with her? Jake was so good and unselfish. He loved her. That was what was important. Nothing else was.

She had no right to pass judgment on him. She didn't know the whole story. There had to be some excuse for the way things looked. She didn't care what people said; she would trust Jake until he proved that she shouldn't. He hadn't done that yet, and she doubted he ever would.

She splashed her face with cool water and drew a deep breath. This weekend was a chance to escape from day-to-day pressures and get to know each other better. She was not going to think about any of her suspicions; instead, she would think about how much they loved each other.

Taking off her slacks and light sweater, she walked back to the bedroom to get her heavier outdoor clothes and saw Jake's eyes light up. He cared about her. She knew he did, and that knowledge made her feel better.

He came up behind her as she rummaged through the suitcase, hugging her around the waist and kissing her on the shoulder. "Very good, madam," he murmured into her hair. "I see the lady would like to indulge in some indoor sports."

She gave him a playful dig in the stomach with her elbow. "No, madam wishes to go hiking and is changing her clothes."

Grunting, he let go of her. She picked up her things and sat on the bed to put on her heavy socks.

"Madam doesn't know her own strength," he said as he rubbed his stomach. "A simple no would have been sufficient."

"Is that right?" she mocked, pulling her jeans on. "I remember somebody once telling me that a woman's no meant maybe."

"It's all a matter of tonal inflection," he grumbled.

Pulling the heavy sweater over her head, Kaye snickered. "I prefer the definite impact of a sharp elbow myself. Besides, we're paying good money for this place, and I don't want to let all that beautiful outdoors go to waste." She tied her shoes and went toward the door. "Come on, lazybones, this was your idea, remember?"

"Actually, I had some other ideas," he pointed out.

"In due time." She forced herself to laugh, then found it wasn't so hard to do. She felt more like herself as she ran down the hallway.

It was beautiful outside. The sun was shining, and it gave a touch of warmth to the cool air. They chose a path leading away from the inn and walked deep into the woods. This was what they needed, some time alone, doing something they both enjoyed. They used to go hiking a lot in the spring and early summer, but then things got busy at the store and they let some of these private moments slip away. They had to be more careful not to do that in the future, Kaye vowed.

They walked slowly along the trail. The leaves were almost all gone from the trees, and the wildlife of the area was clearly visible. Rabbits as still as statues tried to blend into the surroundings. Finches, blue jays, and starlings chattered in the treetops and an occasional cardinal flew by. Far off in a hollow, a family of deer grazed peacefully.

The brisk air and exertion made Kaye feel alive again. The worries were still there, but not hanging like a pall over every thought she had. There was something about the crunch of the leaves beneath her feet that put things into perspective. If Jake was holding something back from her, he must have a good reason. When the time was right, he would clear away all her doubts and fears; she must simply be patient. She smiled lovingly at Jake, and he grinned back at her.

"What's so funny?" she demanded.

"You. When you're out in the cold, your nose gets

all red, and your cheeks turn rosy. Makes you look like a clown."

"Is that right?" She marched toward him with mock menace.

"Uh-oh, Bozo's coming," he teased, and tried to hide behind a tree.

She ran around it and caught up with him, grabbing him from behind and throwing her arms around his waist. "Oh, no, you don't," she said, laughing. "You're not getting away with those remarks. You'll have to pay."

"Who's going to make me?"

"Bozo."

As she held him tightly from behind she let one of her hands find the closure of his shirt and slide inside between the buttons.

"Hey, your hands are cold," he cried.

"Are you sorry you laughed at me?"

"Yes, yes," he said quickly, and squirmed to get away from her icy hands. Once he was free, he turned around, a mischievious gleam in his eye. "I shouldn't have just laughed; I should have tickled you, too."

He darted toward her, and Kaye ran away, laughing as she avoided his hands. She left the path, and he chased after her. It felt so wonderful to run in the crisp air, to feel free and alive again. All her worries seemed far away, unreal.

When her foot slipped on a branch, she fell into a pile of dry leaves. Jake came down next to her, his arms going around her body to hold her close.

"Gotcha!" He laughed and reached over to kiss her soundly. Of their own volition, her arms wound around his neck. The leaves rustled slightly as she rolled onto her back, Jake's weight pinning her down.

He kissed her again, more deeply this time, his tongue exploring the wonders of her mouth as they clung together in rapturous wonder. There was no one in their world but them. The woods, the trees, even the leaves beneath them, vanished as the desires and needs of their bodies took over.

Kaye's hands ran through Jake's softly curly black hair as she held his mouth to hers. She was lost in their own private splendor, her mind swirling. Jake was all that she needed, all that she wanted, and her hands longed to explore every inch of him. It was only when her hand touched a leaf stuck to his shirt that she remembered where they were.

"Maybe we ought to go back to the room," she said softly. "We wouldn't want to shock the rabbits."

"You don't think they know about love?" he teased. "Where do you think all those baby rabbits come from?" He got to his feet and reached his hand down to help her up. Their arms entwined and their bodies touching, they walked back to the inn.

Once in their room, they undressed quickly, still with the same longings pounding through their hearts. Jake took her in his arms and placed her gently on the bed.

This was just what she needed, she thought as her hands touched him gently, lovingly. She could feel the blood race beneath her fingers and the steady rise of his passion. His body responded to her needs, just as she blossomed in response to him.

A hazy fog of pleasure surrounded her. Jake's hands

stoked the fire within her, building it to such an intensity that she felt as if she scorched everything around her. The very sensation of his touch on her skin—her breasts, her thighs—was enough to explode the smoldering desires within her.

As her hunger grew, she took pleasure in arousing his passions. She found his mouth and ran her tongue lightly over his lips. It was a teasing motion, tempting him with promises, but then her tongue refused to go past the lips that so eagerly sought to devour it.

His caresses became rougher and more insistent. His touch was no longer gentle, but an urgent reminder of her power over him. She knew just how to please him with a simple touch of her hand or the flick of her tongue. As he did for her with the pressure of his hair-roughened skin. Even his breath against her neck ignited the conflagration of their love. Without any need for words, their bodies climbed to higher and higher peaks of ecstasy.

"Kaye," he whispered impatiently, and she took him into her womanly recesses.

Their rhythm was perfectly matched. They clung tightly as their spirits soared, and then they relaxed. Tired and comfortable, they clung to each other as the fire dimmed, merely banked and not extinguished, waiting for the next time.

She kissed him on the ear and neck. An involuntary shiver went through her body.

"Cold?" he asked.

"Just my back."

He gently rolled her off and then pulled back the covers. Kaye quickly went under the bed covers with him, lying on top of him again. Her eyes closed momentarily. She was relaxed and happy. Everything seemed right again.

Kaye opened her eyes and felt completely disoriented. The room was totally dark. "Someone turned off all the lights," she said.

Jake laughed quietly. "It's dark out. You've been asleep for over an hour."

She yawned as she felt Jake tenderly roll her over and come on top of her. She felt in a very comfortable and giving mood. His hairy chest felt prickly, and exciting against her body. His need for love quickly came and pierced her sleepy fog with a demanding but gentle force of pleasure.

"My goodness." She laughed. "Do I know you?"

"Quiet, wench," he growled in her ear between light kisses.

Kaye wrapped her legs around him and rode his rhythm, playing entirely to his needs. A slight moan and he came to a shuddering climax, relaxing on top of her. She stretched out her legs, but kept her arms wrapped tightly around him. She liked having him close to her.

Jake shifted his body and raised his head. "I'm hungry."

"That's what I'm here for."

"You insatiable witch." He kissed her, then got out of bed. "I mean food for my stomach."

Kaye got up also and went to take her shower. As the warm water washed over her, she smiled contentedly. They could communicate in so many ways.

They just needed to expand that to include his job. Once they understood each other better, there wouldn't be any more problems. Perhaps now that their intimacy had been reestablished, she could give him an opening. She remembered what the lawyer had said about Jake's older brother. Perhaps if she asked him about Bill...

"Brrr!" Kaye exclaimed as they returned to their room after dinner Sunday evening. "Once that sun goes down, it really gets cold around here."

Jake wrapped his arms around her. "Don't worry about it. Once the sun goes down, I turn my furnace up." He kissed her hair and blew his warm breath on her neck.

Kaye giggled and then squirmed out of his grasp. "I have to blow my nose," she said. "Then I'll slip into something warm and cuddly and come right back out."

He planted one last kiss on her cheek. "Don't be gone long."

Jake kicked his shoes off, sat down in an armchair and put his feet up on the bed. He leaned back and closed his eyes, enveloped in a feeling of contentment. The weekend had done everything he had hoped it would. After some tense moments on Friday, they had regained all that lost ground. They were really a couple again. Loving and caring. Kaye's worries and reservations had been blown away by the brisk autumn winds and some concentrated loving.

At the sound of the bathroom door opening, Jake turned to see Kaye coming out. She had taken the barrettes out of her blond tresses, and her hair hung loose in shining swirls at her shoulders. She was wearing the long, fuzzy bathrobe that he had given her last Christmas and looked like a maroon bear. He watched her, a current of desire warming in him. Even the shapeless, fuzzy robe couldn't hide her desirability.

She put a pillow up against the headboard and then climbed onto the bed. Her feet tucked under her, she wrapped herself securely in the robe, even slipping her hands into the opposite sleeves. About the only skin that showed was her face. It was scrubbed clean of makeup, so that she looked surprisingly young and vulnerable.

Jake felt his need for her grow stronger. "If you're cold, come here. My furnace is stoked up high."

"Why don't you bank it for now? I wouldn't want you to burn out," she said, a soft smile on her lips.

"No problem." He laughed. "It runs on air."

"Is that why you had two pieces of cheesecake for dessert?"

"I'll run it off," he quickly replied.

"I didn't say anything about the horrendous number of calories you took in."

"You were thinking it."

She just smiled.

"Anyway," he said, bouncing on the bed, "as my wife, it's your duty to help me work off those calories."

"And how might I do that?"

"Studies have shown that the act of love compares favorably to climbing six flights of stairs. And," he added, "it's a hell of lot more fun."

Kaye merely grunted, so Jake slid his hand under the robe and moved it toward her feet.

"Get out of there," she exclaimed. "My feet are still cold."

He rolled over on his side and unbuttoned the front of his heavy flannel shirt. Then he pulled her feet out and placed them on his stomach and chest, carefully gathering her robe around them. He started slightly when her feet actually touched him. She hadn't been kidding. They were freezing. After a few minutes, though, they seemed warmer, and she wiggled her toes against him.

"I told you the furnace was going."

Kaye giggled. "It feels like it's set on high."

He smiled, enjoying the feeling of togetherness. After the past week, he wasn't sure how soon they would be able to relax like this. He reached over suddenly and kissed one of her calves, then just as quickly replaced the robe. "I can't resist you, you know."

She smiled, her feet moving slightly against his chest. He slipped a hand under her robe to massage her calves, and she looked at him, her eyes growing soft. He smiled back at her. He read the look in her eyes, and his hand moved to the inside of her thigh.

The eyes lost their softness. "Jake, I want to talk."

After a moment's hesitation, his hand came out. He carefully closed the robe and then looked up at Kaye. "All right."

There was a long period of silence. She looked very serious, and Jake felt an uneasiness in his stomach. Maybe he had been too quick to assume that she had gotten over her moodiness. Maybe it hadn't been blown away but just put aside temporarily.

"Tell me about you brother, Jake. Tell me about Bill."

The uneasiness turned into pain. Active, gut-wrenching pain. Jake swallowed hard and tried to relax his clenched teeth. "What's there to tell? Bill was four years older than I. He was a judge, too—you might say I followed in his footsteps." He fought back the memories during a moment of silence, then added, "And he died a few years ago in an automobile accident."

Kaye was watching him, and he felt the need to look away.

"What kind of judge was he?"

"What's that supposed to mean?" The sharpness in his voice surprised them both, but Kaye didn't say anything.

"Was he in housing court, too?" she asked after a moment.

"Yes."

Another long silence. Then she asked, "Why did you become a judge?"

"Hey, we've been all through this before," he replied, forcing a light, bantering tone into his voice. "You know my father was one. So when Bill died I was appointed to take his place. When Mike gets out of law school, and has a few years of private practice under his belt, he can take over. That's the way we Irish do things. We keep it in the family."

The direction of the conversation scared him. He put his hand under her robe and began rubbing her calf again. Kaye's hands had come out of her sleeves, and she wrapped her arms around her knees as she stared off into space. Her feet were quiet too. It appeared that she wasn't cold anymore. His hand moved up to her thigh again. They didn't need any more conversation. It wouldn't help anything, just hurt.

"We talked about it, I guess, but I still don't understand some things. Like, why does a lawyer become a judge when he can earn so much more in private practice?"

His hand came out again. "A dedication to public service?"

"I imagine there must be a lot of pressures in such a position," she went on quietly.

Jake felt as if he were on the witness stand, and he didn't like it. "What's the purpose of this conversation?"

"I'd like to know about your work. We talk about my job, but we hardly ever talk about yours."

"It isn't all that interesting. Tenants bring complaints against landlords, and I decide if they're valid. I give the landlords a chance to make repairs, and if they don't or won't, they get fined. No big scandals like divorce court, no mystery and intrigue like criminal court." He was growing very tense and tried to force himself to relax.

"I think that's interesting," she protested. "The judgments you make affect everyone's lives."

"My judgments only affect landlords and tenants."

She was going to poke and probe forever until they both were unhappy. There was nothing he could tell her that she wanted to hear, so he'd better put a stop to it. He rolled off the bed and stood up.

"We have to get up early in the morning," he said with an elaborate yawn. "I'm going to hit the sack."

Jake walked quickly into the bathroom, closing the door behind him and leaning against it with a sigh. It was what he had feared all week. She knew. Someone at the damn party must have said something to her, and now she wanted to know the truth from him.

He could only put her off so long. Sooner or later, she was going to come right out and ask him. Was there an answer he could give that would not betray any confidences and still not make her think he was a crook? He couldn't think of one.

He wished he had never started this whole thing. It had seemed so easy at first, but then he had been on his own, with no wife to consider. Now there was Kaye, and she meant everything to him. Yet he had a job to do, a commitment to uphold. He could only hope and pray that Kaye loved him enough to bear with him.

After Jake went into the bathroom, Kaye stayed on the bed, staring at the opposite wall. Maybe she shouldn't have mentioned his dead brother. Maybe that was what upset him. She knew that Jake had been very close to Bill, and even though it had been more than two years since he died, Jake still felt his loss. She wished she could do something to help him get over it, but he always seemed to close her out of that area of his life. His job and Bill were off limits. She didn't know what to do but keep asking questions.

He looked surprised to see her still in the same

place when he came out of the bathroom. His glance seemed uneasy as he walked over to his side of the bed.

"We've always shared things, Jake. Why won't you talk about your job?" she asked him quietly.

"I thought that's what we just did."

Irritation was building, but she took a slow, deep breath before she continued. "We talked about what a housing court judge does, not what *you* do. That's what I want to know. You, as opposed to the things I read in the newspapers and hear on television."

"What kinds of things?"

"Come on, Jake, you know very well what I'm talking about," she snapped impatiently. "About dirty machine politics, about corruption, about how every elected official is on the take."

He stood at the window staring out into the darkness so long that she thought he was not going to answer at all. Finally, he did.

"The public gets exactly what it wants. Corruption and payoffs have been a part of government since its beginning. Periodically, some people get upset because they think they're not getting their share of the loot. So they kick the old crooks out and bring in some new ones. That's a fact of life."

She looked at him, but he didn't turn around. She hugged her knees tightly to her chest.

"What about you, Jake?" The words sounded so loud and accusing; she couldn't believe she had said them.

"Are you asking if I'm on the take?" He turned then, and his eyes seemed sad. "What do you think?"

She was stunned. "What do I think? What should I think? You're my husband and I love you, but I've heard some pretty awful things about you lately."

He came and sat on the bed, reaching across to take her hand. "I guess it all boils down to trust, doesn't it?" he said quietly. "Either you trust me or you don't."

"It's not that simple," she cried, shaking her head. "I love you, but at times I don't think I know you. There's so much of your life that I'm not a part of."

"Nothing that's really important," he said. He moved closer to her, gently pushing the hair from her face in a touching, protective caress. "I'm not so complicated; really I'm not."

"Oh, Jake," she sighed and fell forward into his arms, laying her head against his chest. She felt so safe and secure in his arms, as if the world were far away and would never intrude. Unfortunately, she knew it was only an illusion.

"A lot of people cut corners to make a living," he said suddenly, his voice brisk and matter-of-fact. "Tax attorneys stretch an interpretation of an IRS ruling. Businessmen skim cash from the drawer before they report their income. Doctors collaborate on unnecessary operations. Just about everybody cheats sometimes."

Was he trying to excuse himself? The idea caused her pain. "That doesn't make it right," she pointed out.

His embrace tightened slightly. "Ah, my incorruptible wife," he said, so softly that she wasn't quite sure she'd heard him right. "I'm not so different from you as you think. We both have such a strong sense of honor—maybe more than is good for us, but that's how we are. No wonder we fell in love. Maybe we never spelled it all out, but we're very much the same."

His face was above hers, his eyes tinged with sadness and regret. She reached up and gently stroked the lines of worry from his face.

"I've heard some terrible things about you," she told him softly.

He nodded. "But can you trust in our love?"

"Yes," she whispered. "What we have is real and lasting."

His mouth came down on hers, hard and demanding, but almost pleading, too. She responded to him fully, letting her passions flow in a desperate attempt to erase the memories of those accusations from her mind. Jake was her husband, the man she loved, the man she trusted her life to. She would have faith in him.

Their weekend had been marvelous, renewing in so many ways, yet as the car sped them back to Chicago, Kaye was not at peace. An eerie feeling of doom seemed to hang over their heads. She glanced toward Jake, but his concentration was on his driving. What was wrong with her? Why was she still worried after his comforting of last night?

There was something very wrong happening, but she dared not ask Jake any more about it. She had promised to trust him, and she would. No matter what.

4

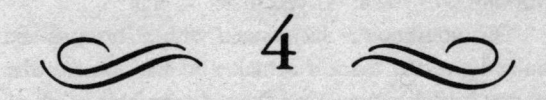

"HAVE YOU TURNED in your expense sheets for that New York fashion show yet?"

Kaye looked up at Jacqui Billows, the manager of ladies' casual wear, the next department over from lingerie. Their tiny offices were right next to each other, and both were adjacent to their departments' narrow storeroom and row of dressing rooms. Unfortunately, even though just a narrow partition separated their offices, there was no easy way to get from one to the other. To get to Kaye's office, Jacqui had had to walk through her own department, around a mannequin display, and past the counters where the bras were stored according to size.

"No, I haven't even thought of expenses yet," Kaye

admitted. "I'm still trying to figure out where half of my Christmas stock has gone. Somewhere out in the main storeroom there must be a hundred nightgowns, robes, and matching slippers."

"Just hope they find them before the after-Christmas reductions start." Jacqui laughed. She sat down next to Kaye's desk and put down her expense record. "I thought we ought to compare our lies so that they match."

"Compare our lies?" Kaye asked. With a frown, she pushed aside the inventory sheets she had been working on. "What do you mean by that?"

"Oh, you know," Jacqui said with a shrug as she walked over to the coffeemaker in the corner. She poured herself a cup, then flipped through a stack of lingerie ads that were pinned to a bulletin board. "I thought we'd get less flak if our expenses sort of matched, for cabs, meals, that kind of stuff." She paused a moment. "Say, you've got some great ads coming up. I love these silk-look lounging pajamas. I may have to get myself a pair when they come in."

Kaye ignored Jacqui's change of subject. "We hardly had any expenses. We didn't pay for a single meal the whole time we were out East, and one of the manufacturer's reps drove us to the airport."

"But accounting doesn't know that," Jacqui said. She brought her coffee over and sat down again. "There are certain expenses that they expect us to have, ones that they'd routinely approve without any question. In fact, they'll probably think it's strange if we don't list them."

"I'll take that chance."

Honorable Intentions

There was a light tap on Kaye's open door, and her assistant manager, Tina, came in. "Sorry to bother you, Kaye, but there's a lady out there who wants to know if we'll take anything off this." She showed Kaye an expensive full slip that had a cigarette burn near the bottom."

"How'd that get there?" Kaye asked.

Tina shook her head.

"This lady have a cigarette in her hand, by any chance?" Kaye asked.

"No," Tina said. "And she's been in the department for a while. She's buying two bras and some panties in addition to the slip."

Kaye nodded and looked again at the burn. It was so close to the seam that an experienced seamstress could make adjustments, but it did ruin a beautiful piece of lingerie. She sighed and gave the garment back to Tina. "Give her the usual damaged goods discount, and get after the salesgirls. I don't want anyone smoking near the merchandise."

Tina nodded and left the office. It was silent for a while. Then Jacqui put her cup down on the edge of the desk.

"The store will lose money on that slip," she pointed out.

Kaye went over to get herself a cup of coffee. "The store always loses money on damaged goods. At least this way, we've got a customer who thinks she got a bargain and might come back to spend more next time."

"You could have charged it against the manufacturer. Maybe the slip got burned at their plant."

"We check over all our merchandise before it goes on the floor, just as you do. There's no way a burn like that could have gotten past us." Kaye sat down. Had Jacqui always been so unprincipled? Why had she never noticed it before?

"The manufacturer wouldn't know."

"Just like accounting?" Kaye got to her feet, suddenly too irritated to sit any longer. "I'm afraid I don't do things that way."

Jacqui rose also. "You're the only one in the world who doesn't, then," she snapped. "Thanks a lot, friend. You just cost me the new dress I was planning to get for Christmas."

Kaye said nothing as she watched her go. Jacqui didn't need extra money from padded expenses to buy anything, but she seemed to think it was her due. Part of her perks. Kaye sighed. Why did it seem that corruption and greed were all around her?

"Are you all right, honey?" Jake sounded concerned as they walked up to his mother's home Thanksgiving Day.

"Yes, of course I am. Why do you ask?"

"You seemed so quiet on the way here, I thought maybe you weren't feeling too well."

"I'm fine," she assured him, and bent her head, pretending to adjust the foil covering on the pie she was carrying. She was still not sure just what was going on in Jake's life, but she thought she had come to terms with the uncertainty. She trusted him and was determined to keep on doing so. But today something else was bothering her.

"I was afraid you were upset about not having Thanksgiving at home," he went on. "But Mom always has us all over."

Kaye laughed at his interpretation of her silence. "Believe me, I don't mind waiting a little longer for my first chance to cook a turkey. I wasn't brooding during the whole ride because of that."

Jake stopped at the foot of the stairs and turned toward her. "Then what *were* you brooding about?"

"Nothing," she snapped impatiently. "I was not brooding. I was just quiet."

"Why? Did somebody say something about me again?"

She didn't have to ask what someone might have said. She understood the reference and wanted to reassure him, to take away that strangely sad look about him. She grabbed at the first excuse that came into her head. "If you must know, I'm worried that my pie will be awful. Your mother probably has some family recipe for pumpkin pie that you all love, and no one will like mine."

Jake laughed and put his arm around her shoulders. Together, they started up the stairs. "Don't be silly. They'll love your pie."

She smiled back at him, and he appeared not to notice that her heart wasn't in it. She hadn't actually been worrying about her pie. His family would probably like it better than they liked her. That was the problem: Kaye had never felt truly accepted by Jake's family. There had even been a slight shadow cast on their wedding day by a remark Jake's sister-in-law Marcia had made to Kaye at the reception.

"Isn't it fortunate the Church has liberalized its rules about marrying Protestants?" she asked Kaye with seeming sincerity. "I'm sure it will make things easier for you with Mom Corrigan that you were married at St. Mary's. None of her other sons ever so much as dated a girl who wasn't Irish, let alone an Episcopalian. But at least you have Father Dowling's blessing, even if some of the parishioners did talk..."

Kaye had been stunned. Jake had never indicated that her background was any problem for him or his family. His mother had been polite to her... and yet she suddenly realized that the other daughters-in-law *were* all Irish Catholics. From then on, she couldn't help feeling like an outsider sometimes, when they referred to "the old country" or made other allusions to a common culture she didn't share.

"Jake, darling. We were wondering when you'd get here," Jake's mother greeted them at the door. "Hello, Kaye. How is it you always look so pretty?"

"I'm not sure I do, but thank you anyway." Kaye smiled at her. "Happy Thanksgiving."

Mrs. Corrigan let them inside, and immediately they were swallowed up in Jake's family. When Kaye had first counted actual numbers, she had been astonished to learn there were fewer than ten adults. It had always seemed like hundreds, all milling about and all talking at once. Thanksgiving was no exception. They were greeted from all directions. Jake's college-age sister, Megan, was on the phone, but covered the receiver long enough to shout a greeting. Marcia's husband, Danny, took their coats, while Marcia herself reached for Kaye's pie.

"I can take it into the kitchen," Kaye protested weakly.

"Don't be silly. Just because we're trapped in there is no reason you ought to be. After all, you're a guest."

No, she wasn't, Kaye thought angrily. She was family, too. Just as much family as Marcia was. Only not for as long.

She didn't say her thoughts aloud, though, as Marcia peeked under the foil at her pie. "It looks delicious. Better than mine ever did."

"See?" Jake smiled at her, just as Kaye had feared he would. "I told you not to worry about it."

"Worry about what?" his mother asked.

Before Kaye could introduce a new subject, Jake went on, "Kaye was worried we wouldn't like her pie. She was afraid her recipe wouldn't be like yours."

Forcing herself to smile despite her embarrassment, Kaye accepted the Corrigans' assurances that they would love her pie.

"We'll especially love it since you went to the trouble of making it," Marcia said a little too sweetly. "I'm surprised you had time, what with working such long hours and all."

Kaye caught the implication, even though no one else seemed to: Marcia was a full-time housewife, and since Kaye wasn't, she obviously wasn't as competent in domestic matters.

"She had the time to bake because she neglected me," Jake pointed out.

There was a chorus of sympathetic cries as his mother shooed them all into the living room. She and Marcia went on toward the kitchen.

Kaye followed them. "Is there something I can do to help?"

Mrs. Corrigan looked uncertain. "That's sweet of you to offer," she said, and glanced toward Marcia.

"But we really have everything in hand," Marcia finished for her. "And we'd hate to see you get that pretty dress all dirty." She patted Kaye on the arm. "Just go back in with the others and enjoy yourself. Tell Jake to fix you two something to drink." She went through the swinging door and into the kitchen.

"Why don't you get Jake to show you the family album?" Mrs. Corrigan suggested. "I think you'd get a kick out of seeing some of the pictures in it."

Kaye nodded with a smile, then walked slowly back into the living room where Jake and Danny were sitting. Three of Danny's kids ran through the room, arguing about something. Kaye took a seat next to Jake and squeezed his hand. He paused briefly in his conversation to smile at her.

She never quite felt as if she belonged here, Kaye thought, her mind wandering from the discussion of the traditional Thanksgiving Day football games. Mrs. Corrigan was nice, but Kaye always wondered if the religious difference was bothering her. And others never seemed to welcome Kaye at all. Everyone was always terribly polite, and she had nothing concrete to put her finger on, but they treated her like a guest, not like family. How long would it take before they really accepted her?

Marcia came into the room, an apron tied around her waist as she called Danny into the kitchen to take the turkey out of the oven so they could baste it.

Marcia was really the worst, Kaye thought as she watched the short, plump woman go back toward the kitchen. She was the one who always seemed to exclude Kaye and make remarks that made Kaye feel like an outsider.

The doorbell rang and interrupted the football talk. Jake went to answer it. It was his younger brother Mike and his wife, Lucy. Marcia and Mrs. Corrigan came in from the kitchen, and the usual uproar of hugs and kisses surrounded their arrival. But Lucy was swept along to the kitchen with the other women, not left behind as Kaye had been.

Kaye stayed in the living room only a moment after the others had left for the kitchen. Then she picked up a few empty glasses that were in sight and marched after them. She was Jake's wife, and they were going to accept her. If she could work effectively enough with businessmen in the merchants' association to be nominated for president, she could manage Jake's brothers and sisters.

"I've brought in some dirty glasses," she announced. "Shall I put them in the dishwasher?"

"Oh, no. You don't have to bother," Marcia said. "Just leave them on the counter. We'll put them away later."

Kaye stood holding the glasses for a moment, uncertain what to do. She hated to make an issue of it. Maybe she was expecting things to happen too fast. Lucy and Marcia had been in the family for years, not months. Maybe she was being impatient. She looked up and found Mrs. Corrigan smiling at her.

"I don't know about anybody else," Mrs. Corrigan

announced, "but I feel overworked enough on Thanksgiving. If Kaye wants to put a few glasses in the dishwasher, I'll be grateful for her help."

Marcia looked surprised, then defensive. "I just didn't want to see her get her dress dirty."

The atmosphere seemed rather tense to Kaye, but Mrs. Corrigan didn't seem bothered by it. "How about if she sets the table, then?"

Marcia shrugged rather helplessly, then led Kaye into the dining room. "I'll show her where everything is."

Kaye followed her, wondering why Marcia was so antagonistic. What had she ever done to make her that way?

Marcia took a tablecloth and some napkins out of a cabinet. Kaye took one end and helped her spread it out.

"How many of us will there be?" Kaye asked.

"Eleven." Marcia went to the china cabinet and began to take pieces out.

"Then Peggy and her son aren't coming?" Jake had told her that Bill's widow and son sometimes spent Thanksgiving with his family.

Marcia shook her head, watching Kaye strangely. "Has Jake talked to you much about Bill?" she asked.

"No." Kaye was surprised that Marcia mentioned him so casually. No one else ever did, and from the whole family's strange attitude, she had begun to suspect that no one was allowed to.

"I was surprised when you mentioned Peggy. I thought maybe Jake had finally come to terms with what Bill did."

"What he did?" Kaye was really confused. "What did Bill do?"

Marcia laughed harshly. "Don't tell me you haven't heard the whole sordid story! You've been a Corrigan for eight months. I thought you'd be sick of it by now."

Seeing Marcia's bitterness, Kaye was not sure she wanted to know what "the whole sordid story" was.

"Bill and Jake were very close," Marcia told her. "I sometimes think he took Bill's death harder than any of us. He just didn't seem able to put the whole awful mess behind him."

"You mean Bill's accident?"

"No, not that. Anybody can have a car accident. I mean the scandal they uncovered afterward."

Oh, Lord. Something told her that she didn't want to hear this, but all she could do was dumbly shake her head. Marcia sat down with a sigh at the head of the table. Kaye sat down next to her.

"After Bill's death, irrefutable evidence of corruption was uncovered in his records," Marcia told her.

"Corruption?" Kaye whispered.

"Bribe-taking, fixed decisions. A whole bunch of things." Marcia looked away, and her voice sounded angry. "His mother wouldn't believe it at first, but the proof was all there. It just took her a little while to accept it. The rest of us believed it right away. You see, we had all grown up in Bill's shadow. We had known for years that no one could be that perfect."

The contempt in Marcia's voice startled Kaye. "Who said he was perfect?" Kaye asked.

Marcia shrugged. "Everybody thought he was. His

parents acted as if the sun rose and set on his every word. It got a little tiresome at times, believe me. Somebody like Danny, who's just a quiet guy, never got any attention."

That explained some of Marcia's anger, Kaye thought. She didn't like her sister-in-law any better, but at least she began to understand her. It must have been hard for Marcia to see her husband constantly taking second place to his brother. "How did Jake take the news about Bill's corruption?"

"Worse than the rest of us. No one could talk to him about it or reason with him. I guess, as a lawyer, he found he couldn't argue with the evidence, yet he had believed the saintly myth, too." Marcia got to her feet. "We just find now it's easier not to mention Bill at all. Mom Corrigan is starting to appreciate her other sons more, so why drag up the past?"

Kaye nodded as Marcia left the room; then she finished setting the table in silence. Jake had asked her to trust him, and she would. No matter what Marcia thought of Bill, Kaye was not going to make any such judgments about Jake.

Jake bent over the VCR and rewound the tape. His mother refused to turn the TV on during family dinners, so he'd taped the Lions game. What was Thanksgiving without football?

He had been troubled at dinner to hear that Peggy was remarrying. He knew the prick of resentment he'd felt was irrational, but he couldn't help it. Bill wasn't dead for him, especially now . . .

The tape stopped rewinding, and he pushed the

button for it to start. The network sportscasters were horsing around as he sat down. The game would begin in a moment.

Jake sighed. More than two years had passed since the accident. Peggy was young and deserved happiness, not a bunch of memories, and Billy could sure use a father. But still, it hurt him like hell to see them replace Bill in their lives.

Was he jealous? he wondered. He had wanted to take care of them after Bill's death, but then all those rumors had surfaced, and Peggy had fled. How could he be a surrogate father to Billy when he was a hundred miles away?

The national anthem floated out into the room, and then the teams lined up on the field. Detroit kicked off, and their opponents dropped the ball. The game seemed less than exciting.

He went to the kitchen to get a beer, and when he came back Detroit had possession at their own forty-yard line. Jake shook his head. This was some game. He probably ought to turn the dumb thing off. He took a long drink and sat down.

Would Kaye react as Peggy had? he wondered. If she had the chance, would she run away from all the rumors? He didn't know. He hoped not. He thought Kaye was stronger than Peggy. But things were liable to get rougher before they got better, and he didn't think he could bear it if Kaye ran away.

He wished he could have talked to Peggy about Bill, about the Bill he knew. The one who never would have taken bribes or done anything even halfway wrong. But she had frozen when all that had come out. She wouldn't talk to him or let him reassure her. She had run away. Was she getting married again to try to erase her memories of Bill? Perhaps that suspicion was what hurt him the most.

One of Detroit's running backs made a beautiful run, and the Lions were close to scoring. Who cares? Jake thought. He leaned back in the chair and closed his eyes.

Peggy had said that there were too many memories in this town. Both she and Billy needed a new start. Life was for the living. Jake couldn't argue. He'd remembered his father saying that when he learned he had cancer.

No doubt, Peggy's fiancé was a fine man, he told himself. It was just that Jake wanted to pay Bill back for all that he had done for him. Jake owed him a lot, and the least he could do was clear his name. He heard Kaye sit down on the sofa across from him, and he opened his eyes.

"How's the game?" she asked.

"Boring." He got up and went over to sit next to her. Her eyes looked so grave lately. He wished there was some way to get that sparkle of happiness back into them. He missed her teasing ways and the sound of her laughter.

He kept telling himself that she just needed more time, but how much time? Would she be strained and hurt until his part in all this was over? It looked now as if that could be years. He didn't think he could bear to see her suffer for that long.

He put his arm around her shoulders, and she rested her head against his chest with a tired sigh. He hugged

Honorable Intentions 67

her a little tighter and planted a quick kiss on her hair.

"Did you have a nice day?" he asked.

"Sure. I really like your mother." She was silent a moment, then added, "I think I would have liked Bill, too."

"Yeah." Damn. Why couldn't he tell her about his brother? Tell her what a great guy he was and how close they had been as kids. About Bill teaching him to play baseball and helping him with his homework, and never minding his younger brother tagging along. About how much he loved him. Maybe because if he started, he'd tell her everything. He couldn't do that. He decided instead to take comfort from her in other ways.

He held her close and kissed her neck tenderly. He had never thought he could love someone as much as he loved Kaye. It almost scared him, this power that she held over him.

His hand delved inside her blouse and under her bra. Her breast was soft and warm and responsive to his touch. She cuddled closer to him, kissing the side of his neck as she leaned her head against his. He felt his body surge with need for her.

Kaye slipped her hand under his shirt and ran it over his chest. Her touch was gentle and soothing, making him forget the worries of the day. The roar of the crowd from the television set barely penetrated his consciousness, but he felt Kaye turn to glance at the set.

"One of the blue players just scored a touchdown," she told him.

"I don't think I care anymore."

She smiled, and he ran his hand over her back, stopping on her hip. He tightened his embrace, wondering how he had managed before they met. She was so important to him. His whole world revolved around her now. Or at least it would after he had paid his debt to Bill...

5

JAKE SIPPED AT his coffee even though it was too cold to be palatable. Breakfast was over, and Kaye had almost finished reading the newspaper. If he didn't say something soon, he was going to lose his chance.

He cleared his throat, then forced the words out. "You know, you don't really have to come with me today."

Kaye didn't even look up. "That's okay. I don't mind."

"I know you don't mind, but it seems like a pretty boring way for you to spend your day off."

She looked up then, a smile on her lips. "By spending it with you? You don't rate yourself very high."

He got up and went to the sink, giving his full

attention to rinsing out his cup. "It's not as if we'll be together all that much, though. You know, I'll have to circulate and wish everybody a Merry Christmas, and most of those guys aren't really your type." He was grasping at straws, and she seemed to sense it. Her frown was very eloquent.

"If you don't want me to go to this Christmas party with you for some reason, just say so, Jake."

He didn't, really, but with that hurt tone in her voice, what could he say? "It's not that," he said lamely and poured himself another cup of coffee.

"I've never met most of your political associates, and I thought this would be a good chance to do so," she said quietly.

He nodded. They were aware that they hadn't met her, too, and were pushing for it. So she wanted to go and they wanted her to come; but he wished to hell he could prevent it.

Things had been getting a bit sticky lately. He had been so careful at first to play his part to the fullest. He was the big spender who liked to have a good time. But since his marriage to Kaye, he had not been as active. In order to allay the suspicions that Hrljic had begun expressing openly, Jake had allowed the man to think that Kaye had expensive tastes and that he still was just as eager for some extra cash.

Now, if Kaye came to the Christmas party today, she could blow that whole image. Hrljic would stop steering lucrative cases his way, and Jake would cease to be useful. And Jake didn't want Kaye to see him in the role that had been given to him, especially since he couldn't tell her what it was all about. But since she was determined to go to the party with him, he would have to give her some kind of preparation.

He cleared his throat. "Kaye, this party may not be exactly what you're expecting."

She laughed. "How do you know what I'm expecting?"

"Well..." He paused, groping for words. "I'm just saying, whatever happens, however strange anything may seem to you... just keep the faith, okay?"

"Jake, for heaven's sake, what are you talking about? Look, are you afraid your political friends won't approve of me? Am I so different from the other wives—"

"Only that you're head and shoulders above them," he interrupted quickly, grieved to think she might suppose he was ashamed of her.

"Well, then, if you're convinced I won't disgrace you, I'd better get dressed." Kaye stood up and carried her empty cup to the dishwasher. "I suppose we'll be leaving in a half-hour or so?"

"Somewhere around there."

Jake had a sudden idea and watched in thoughtful silence as Kaye walked across the kitchen and down the hall to their bedroom. She had such a regal walk and could have been a model with her polished, graceful presence. She could make old jeans and a sweatshirt look like formal wear. He followed into the bedroom.

"What are you going to wear?"

Kaye had started to take out her makeup and looked into the mirror at his reflection "What am I wearing?" she repeated in confusion. "Does it matter?"

"Well, I was hoping you'd get kind of dressed up."

Kaye stared at him, and he felt uneasy. He shouldn't be getting her involved like this.

"Is there something special you'd like me to wear?" She seemed almost afraid to ask.

That was just the chance he'd been waiting for. "There are a few of your dresses I particularly like," he said and went into their walk-in closet.

"A dress?" She followed him. "It's cold out. I was thinking of a pantsuit."

That would never do. "Some of these guys are rather old-fashioned and—"

"All right," she said quickly and went over to her dresses. "How about this one?" It was a pretty dark red shirtwaist. "Or this one?" she asked about a violet two-piece knit.

"Actually, I like this one."

He took out a deep blue silk that was trimmed with bright green along the bodice and the collar. It also just happened to be the most expensive dress in her closet and looked it. Of course she had used her employee discount and had gotten a further reduction because there was a slight flaw in the fabric under the right arm. But no one else would know that.

"Don't you think that's a bit much for an afternoon luncheon?" she asked.

"I think it's gorgeous," Jake said, putting on his best little-boy smile.

She frowned.

"It's my favorite of all your clothes," he went on. "Except maybe that white negligee."

"I'll be overdressed," she told him. "Everyone will think I'm showing off."

"Nobody else will know how much it cost. You can tell stuff like that because you're in retailing, but most people can't. They'll just think you look beautiful."

"Jake."

He continued to smile hopefully, until she sighed and took the dress from him. "All right, but if nobody will talk to me, it's your fault."

"Just trust me," he said. "No matter what you think, trust me."

She gave him a strange look, so he hurriedly began to select his own clothes, hoping to delay her questions. He took his suit and a shirt into the bedroom. "How about if you wear your diamond pendant, too?" he called back in to her.

Kaye rode to the party in silence. She really was confused. Earlier this morning, she had thought Jake didn't want her at the party; then, abruptly, he seemed determined to make her the center of attention. What was going on?

The closer they got to the south side union hall where the party was to be held, the more oppressive was her sense of doom. Something was wrong; she knew that. She had tried not to think about Jake and those rumors, but had only been briefly successful. Every time it seemed she was finally starting to put her doubts behind her and really trust him, something else happened to frighten her. Why wouldn't Jake tell her what was going on? He kept saying she should keep the faith, but where was his faith in her? Shouldn't trust be a two-way street?

The party was in full swing by the time they got there. They hadn't even taken their coats off before people were greeting Jake.

"Hey, Jake, baby! How ya been, kid?" A tall, balding man came rushing up to him.

Jake slapped him on the back and shook his hand. "Charlie, good to see you. How ya been, buddy?" He turned toward Kaye and put his arm around her shoulders. "I don't think you've ever met my ball and chain, have you?"

His ball and chain? Kaye just stared at Jake in astonishment as she murmured some vague courtesies to Charlie. Since when had he started referring to her as his ball and chain?

"Looks like a good-sized crowd," Jake said.

Charlie laughed. "Yeah, just saying Merry Christmas to half the people here will parch your throat. Better wet your whistle first thing. The bar's way the hell over on the other side of the room."

Charlie must not know Jake all that well, Kaye thought. Jake was a very light drinker.

"You always did have your priorities in order, Charlie." Jake laughed.

Kaye frowned in confusion.

"I just know you judges," Charlie said. "All that pressure develops a powerful thirst in a man."

"Yeah," Jake replied. "You might call it a thirst for justice."

Charlie snickered. "A thirst for Justice Jim Beam?"

Jake roared in laughter as he slapped Charlie on the back again. At the same time, he took Kaye's arm and moved quickly toward the coatroom.

Kaye wasn't able to do more than nod in Charlie's direction. Where was the quiet, reserved man with grace and charm who had accompanied her to other parties? This loud, raucous man couldn't be her husband. She had thought Charlie didn't know Jake, but she was coming to wonder if she might not be the one who didn't know him.

Jake put their coats away while she waited next to a Christmas tree. The other women she saw were dressed up, but not really as ostentatiously as she was. There were other dresses, but certainly no other silk ones. She felt self-conscious and wondered if she should slip her pendant inside her dress. Jake came up and took her arm, leading her inside the hall.

"Jake! How ya doing, old man?" A round little man hurried up to him.

"Not too well." Jake laughed. "We haven't made it to the bar yet."

"Poor lad. I did notice a terrible tremor to your limbs. I'd best not delay you."

"You're damn right. Another two seconds and I'll trample you." Then, still chuckling loudly, Jake turned and introduced Kaye to Bobby LaFountain, the county clerk.

"How do you do?" she answered politely. She had given up being surprised by Jake's comments.

"Can't complain. Wouldn't do any good anyway." He laughed uproariously at his own joke. "Uh-oh, the missus has spotted me. I'd better keep moving or she'll be catching me. Have a good time, you folks."

He was gone before Kaye had a chance to say anything. Meanwhile, Jake had hailed several other people and introduced them to her. She barely caught their names, but there was a great deal of loud laughing and joking about liquor before they went on their way. She and Jake went straight to the bar.

What was going on? Were there two Jakes: the quiet one with a sense of honor and scruples whom she had fallen in love with, and then the politician? Was he some kind of chameleon who tried to be all things to all men, doing whatever was expedient at the moment with no real self to be true to?

Jake called the bartender over as if he expected an immediate response. He got one. Everyone seemed to know him and be willing to jump when he spoke. Slightly unnerved, Kaye ordered a glass of white wine, while Jake ordered a whiskey. That wasn't like him either. He was strictly a beer and wine drinker when he did drink. She was beginning to think she had wandered into a dream.

A short, ruddy-faced man suddenly took Kaye's hand. "Ah, Mrs. Corrigan," he said. "Jake's been bragging about your loveliness all over the town, and I had to see you with my own eyes."

Kaye just stared down at him, feeling like a giant in her high heels. "Jake's always talking," she said.

"Yeah," the man replied. "But in this case, he doesn't do you justice. Only a poet could begin to describe your loveliness. You're a splendid queen amid us peasants."

Honorable Intentions 77

The flowery adulation was beginning to embarrass her. Kaye could feel her cheeks warming.

Jake interrupted. "This is Hank Sullivan, Kaye."

"You're a credit to the Corrigans, my dear," Hank said, kissing her hand. "And by far the loveliest."

"You know Jake's family?"

"Jake, haven't you ever mentioned me to your wife? Well, never mind, guess I wouldn't trouble a goddess like this with the dull details of politics myself." Hank laughed and turned back to Kaye. "I worked with Bill, but I'd take Jake over him. He's the brains of the family."

"Oh?" Kaye glanced over at Jake and was surprised that he had no reaction to his brother's name.

Hank went on. "Hasn't he ever told you about our visits to the track and our nights on the town? Of course, all done before he met you," Hank added. "We're hoping, though, that you'll let him out now and then once the honeymoon's over. Nobody could pick those horses like Jake could."

Jake betting on horses? "He's certainly free to go with you if that's what he wants," Kaye said stiffly.

"Oh, you've done it." Jake laughed and threw a playful punch at Hank. "I managed to keep my colorful past from her until now. I may be joining you sooner than you think if she throws me out."

"Oh, she'd never do that, would you, Kaye?" Hank said. "I can see in her eyes that she loves you." He looked at Jake. "But maybe she'd let you join us at the races if you promise to buy her a mink with your winnings."

"I could try, I suppose," Jake laughed. "But I'd better win big. I have the feeling she'd insist on a full-length Russian one."

Kaye forced herself to join Jake and Hank in their laughter, but was rapidly losing her sense of humor. She didn't like Hank Sullivan one bit, and Jake seemed to be stooping to the slimy little man's level.

"She's just one smart lady, aren't you, Kaye, honey? Don't give him any freedom until he comes across with a few trinkets. Make him pay for what he wants."

Kaye forced a smile to her face. "I don't make Jake pay," she said quietly.

Jake's laugh was loud. "See how well she does it," he said to Hank. "She's got me convinced that I don't *have* to shower furs and jewelry on her to keep her happy; I just do it because I *want* to."

Kaye was stunned. What was Jake saying? She never asked or even hinted for presents. Why was he making her sound so mercenary? She blinked back tears of pain, feeling suddenly alone and abandoned.

Her hand brushed against her necklace, and even that took on new meaning. She had thought when he gave it to her that it was a beautiful romantic gesture. Now she was not so certain. Maybe it was all part of his plan to make her seem shallow and breedy. But why? She no longer felt certain of anything, and through a haze of anguish, she saw Hank pick up her hand and kiss it.

"Ah, lovely, lovely. I'll be taking a vision home with me tonight." He winked at Kaye and then whispered hoarsely out of the side of his mouth to Jake. "My wife's visiting her sister in Cleveland, so it'll be all right." He dashed quickly away.

Jake shook his head with a laugh, as if Hank's presence had been a refreshing treat. "Want to get something to eat?"

Kaye shrugged vaguely, but Jake wasn't even watching for her reply. He took her arm possessively and led her across to the food tables. Their progress was not very fast as Jake constantly stopped to greet people with a vulgar heaviness that Kaye found repellent. Her smile felt stiff and strained. Although Jake always introduced her, most of the conversation revolved around their political connections or her spending habits, and she felt paralyzed by shock and confusion.

She felt sick and betrayed by the time they reached the buffet. How could Jake act this way? He kept asking her to trust him, and she had. And this was how he repaid that trust! She had never been so devastated by hurt.

Although the spread of food literally took her breath away, Kaye was not tempted by any of it. She didn't care that there were delicacies representing almost every ethnic group in the city—Italian sausage, tiny burritos, sauerkraut and sausage, egg rolls, and many other items she didn't even recognize. Jake went ahead of her, filling his plate to overflowing. She took a few things for appearances' sake, but ended up just picking at them while Jake wolfed down everything he had chosen.

"What's the matter, honey? Not hungry?" he asked suddenly, his eyes on her plate.

"Sure, I'm just getting started," she lied. "But if

you want dessert, go ahead. I doubt that I'll have room for any."

He seemed to believe her and was starting to rise when a slender man with iron-gray hair came over to them. The man's lips were smiling, but his eyes seemed hard as coal. "Jake, how are you?"

Jake got to his feet and shook the man's hand. "Johnny, I was wondering if you were coming." He turned to Kaye. "I don't think you've met my wife. Kaye, this is Johnny Hrljic. Johnny, Kaye. I'm sure you remember my speaking of her."

"Yes, indeed," Johnny said, and Kaye was pretty certain she knew what kind of things Jake had been saying. The man noticed her untouched plate. "What's wrong, Mrs. Corrigan? Don't you like our food?"

"I just wasn't very hungry," she said quietly.

"I thought it was great," Jake said. "But Kaye's used to the Pump Room."

Jake's implication that she would have preferred more expensive and richer foods was quite obvious. Certainly, Mr. Hrljic understood it. Kaye's sick feeling of betrayal grew.

"I need to borrow your husband for a few minutes, Mrs. Corrigan," Mr. Hrljic said. "Some dull city business."

Jake wasn't pleased to see Johnny Hrljic, but had expected him to show up sooner or later. He hid his true feelings and smiled up at the man from his seat. "Sure thing, Johnny. You'll excuse us, won't you Kaye?"

Honorable Intentions 81

He didn't wait for her response but followed the other man out into the lobby. It was fairly quiet there.

"Something wrong?" Jake asked.

"Should there be?"

Jake said nothing but waited as Johnny took out a cigarette and lit it. He took a long draw on it, then leaned against the wall. His eyes were on some teenage girls in the doorway to the hall.

"There's been some talk lately that you ought to know about," Johnny said quietly.

"Oh?"

"Hank recognized a new prosecutor in traffic court. He's a Fed."

Jake caught his breath, then let it out slowly. "Is Hank sure?"

Johnny's eyes came back to Jake. "Hank's no dummy. He knows what's coming down."

"Sure, but just because the guy once worked for the Feds—"

"Not *once* worked, *is* working," Johnny corrected sharply. "He's a mole, and there must be others."

Jake was silent for a long time. "Any ideas of who?" he finally asked.

He didn't like Johnny's smile. "You'd know better than me."

A cold fear clutched at Jake's stomach, but his eyes glared at the other man. "What's that supposed to mean?"

Johnny shrugged easily. "Hey, you're the one out there making the money. I'm strictly a behind-the-scenes man. Anybody you suspect?"

"Everybody," Jake snapped.

Johnny smiled. "I always knew you were smarter than your brother."

"Wealthier, too."

"Better stay that way if you plan to keep your missus happy. She doesn't look like the type to stay around too long if you qualify for food stamps." Johnny dropped his cigarette and ground it out with his toe. Then, without even a nod, he went back into the hall.

Jake walked over to the door and stared out at the street. He took a deep breath and let it out, fogging up the glass before him. He had to relax; he had to fight the anger. This wasn't the time or place to get into a showdown with anybody. There'd come a time and a place. He just had to be patient.

That wasn't easy, though, especially not with scum like Johnny. He felt dirty just associating with the man. He hoped it wouldn't be for much longer. He glanced down at his watch. They had been at the party for a couple of hours. He'd get Kaye and leave.

6

KAYE STARED BLINDLY out the window as Jake drove them home. She could not take any more. Jake was going to tell her the truth when they got home. She would insist on it. She wasn't going to go through another moment feeling abused and betrayed as she had this afternoon. Anything would be better than not knowing.

Jake parked the car, and they walked into the house in silence. He had been more subdued on the drive home. Was he aware of how his behavior had hurt her? Why, then, hadn't he said anything, given any small sign of comfort?

The cats were waiting in the kitchen for them, and immediately demanded to be fed. Jake went past them into the living room.

"Jake, I want to talk," she called after him.

"Sure, honey," he said easily, as if he were expecting a discussion of the weather. Unbelievably, she heard the sound of the television warming up. "I just want to see if the De Paul game is still on."

A basketball game! Didn't he have any notion how upset she was? She tossed her coat on the kitchen table, grabbed a can of cat food from the shelf, and opened it quickly.

"Is there corruption in our housing courts?"

Jake stared at the television screen, his blood suddenly running cold. He watched in horror as the announcer went on, accompanied by the films of a burning building.

"Earlier this week," the man said, "this sixteen-unit apartment building was destroyed by fire, leaving over seventy people homeless and twelve poeple hospitalized, four in serious condition. Channel Nine News learned today that the day before the fire, the owner of this building apdeared in housing court in a suit brought by his tenants, but the case was postponed. We also learned that this was the fourteenth time a continuance had been granted in this case. The judge? John Corrigan."

Somewhere off in the distance Jake heard the phone ring, but could not move. He could not take his eyes from the screen. This had always been his greatest fear: that someone would be hurt because of his actions. No matter how carefully he tried to monitor his continuances and make sure no really dangerous situations were left unresolved, he had always feared

Honorable Intentions

he'd make a mistake somewhere.

It was a risk he'd had to take as part of his undercover work for the Justice Department.

He had once tried to talk to Brad Howard, his contact agent, about his fear, but Brad had waved it aside, exhorting Jake to remember the "big picture." Brad had not been concerned about the little people who might lose their homes or their lives; the ends justified the means for him, and Jake had to concede that ultimately more property and lives would be protected if he played his role as Brad advised.

"Jake?" He spun around and saw that Kaye had come into the room.

"There was a reporter on the phone and he said..."

Her voice died away as her eyes went past him to the television set. His picture had been flashed on the screen. It was an old film from some political dinner, showing him laughing and smiling. Quite a contrast to the picture of the homeless people they had just shown. Kaye's face was pale, and her eyes reflected his own horror.

He felt sick to his stomach as the announcer's voice droned on, giving details of other buildings, other continuances that they had discovered. Other people who had suffered because of Jake's decisions. Maybe their homes hadn't been lost, but they were living in fire traps. Some without heat or adequate plumbing. The accompanying pictures were vivid reminders of the price others were paying while the investigation dragged on.

"Damn," he said quietly, feeling their pain and his own frustration. When would it be over?

"Jake, what is going on?" Kaye asked him.

He turned toward her and was faintly surprised to see that she looked angry. In his own agony, he hadn't thought how this all must look to her.

"You told me that you were just a housing court judge. That you never released murderers onto the streets." Her voice was quiet with suppressed emotion, but grew in strength with her anger. "No, you didn't say murderers, did you? You said convicted felons. And an irresponsible landlord doesn't face a murder charge, even if people die because of his neglect, does he? Are you going to make that same distinction to the people in the hospital?"

He just shook his head, not knowing what to say. "Trust me, Kaye. It's not what it seems."

"Trust you?" The words seemed to explode out of her in anger and bitterness. "Trust you, after that fiasco of a party this afternoon? After you let people's homes be burned down around them?"

She sounded so bitter and condemning that he grew afraid. Did she really believe he would knowingly endanger human lives? Had she come to the end of her belief in him? "Just ride this out with me, Kaye. Please."

"Ride it out with you? You make it sound like a storm! Jake, I thought I married a man who believed in justice for all, not an opportunist who sold it to the highest bidder."

He took a step toward her, his hand outstretched, but she pulled back away from his touch. That hurt more than her words.

"The man I married would fight, Jake. He'd light

a candle in the darkness." The tears were flowing down her cheeks now. "He wouldn't steal the damn matches."

What could he say to her? Two years of work. His brother's good name. The cause Bill had sacrificed his reputation for. That bastard Hrljic behind bars where he belonged. So much depended on his silence. The phone began to ring again.

"It'll be doing that all night now," he said. "I'd better put the answering machine on."

Without risking a glance at her face, he hurried from the room. He stopped a moment in the hallway to take a deep, steadying breath. Then he went into the study to turn on the machine.

Nothing was working out as he had expected. He had hoped the investigation would be over soon after they got married, but of course it wasn't. That had just been the first of his pipe dreams. He had hoped Kaye wouldn't hear any rumors; he had hoped no one would be hurt by his actions; he had hoped he could clear Bill's name and fulfill Bill's mission.

Damn! He leaned his hands on the surface of the desk, and took a deep breath. All that he hoped to accomplish... and what had he done so far? Just hurt people. Perhaps Kaye most of all.

But if he told her the truth, he could jeopardize the success of the investigation. At the very least, he'd drag her into the mud with him. Still, after the publicity about the fire, wouldn't she be dragged into it anyway? Reporters would hound him, and she'd get her share. With all the terrible rumors and innuendos that would circulate about him, would she be able to keep in mind how much he loved her and how much they'd shared? What if the strain proved to be too much for her and she left him? How could he bear that?

In the beginning, he had thought his task would be much simpler and more straightforward—root out the corrupt and then go on living. He had known that his reputation would be tarnished for a while; that was inevitable. But he had never thought the dirt would spill over onto Kaye. He had never wanted that.

Yet in spite of his wishes, she was already involved, with only a failing belief in him to support her. If he told her the truth, at least they would have each other. The thought was comforting. But he mustn't be selfish—if he confided in her, it must be for *her* sake, not his own. And he just didn't know anymore... there seemed to be no way to protect her. He closed his eyes and made a silent prayer for guidance.

Kaye paced the room impatiently, waiting for Jake to return. How long did it take to turn on the answering machine? Or was he using that as an excuse to avoid her a little longer? She turned off the television set, unable to hear any more of the accusations, and sat down.

What had happened to the man she thought she married? The fine, upstanding, decent man? Had she just dreamed him up, or was Jake a superbly accomplished actor? Maybe she had fallen in love with an image, a naive vision of what a judge was supposed to be...

Jake came in, and she jumped to her feet. "For godsake, Jake, talk to me," she pleaded without giving him a chance to speak. "If you're in some sort of trouble, I'll stand by you. But not in ignorance. You've got to tell me what's going on. I don't care if you've followed in Bill's footsteps. Just be honest with me for a change."

Her reference to Bill seemed to trigger something in him. He crossed over to her in a few steps and grabbed hold of her arms. "Bill never did anything shameful," he cried. "And neither have I."

She was stunned by his sudden anger, and apparently, so was he. Realizing how hard he had gripped her arms, he released them and sheepishly turned away.

"Neither have I, Kaye," he repeated in a broken whisper. "No matter how it looks, I haven't done a blessed thing wrong. Nothing illegal, nothing immoral. Kaye..."

She was thoroughly confused. "Jake?" She touched his arm gently, but he wouldn't turn around.

"Jake, don't clam up now," she cried impatiently. Didn't he think their marriage was worth fighting for? "Jake, what are you saying?"

He took a deep breath and turned around slowly. "I'm collecting evidence for the Justice Department," he said. "I have to appear to be crooked to uncover the corruption in the courts."

She felt stunned, as if all the breath had been knocked from her body. Collecting evidence? Jake was working undercover? That possibility had never crossed her mind. Her confusion came out in a frown.

Jake must have thought that she didn't believe him.

"It's true," he insisted. "But I wasn't supposed to tell you. So I can't give you a number in Washington to call for verification—you'll just have to take my word for it."

"I believe you." But she had so many questions, she didn't know where to start. She sat down on the edge of the sofa, still feeling dazed. Jake sat next to her. She took his hand in hers.

"What about Bill?" she asked.

He shook his head. "He was working with the Feds, too, but when he was killed in the accident, they couldn't clear his name without blowing the whole operation. I agreed to take his place and got myself appointed to his seat. It wasn't hard to do. Hrljic thought I'd be just as easy to maneuver as Bill was." Jake ended with a bitter little laugh.

Kaye said nothing for a long moment, just holding his hand tightly while she tried to sort out her own confused thoughts.

"Was that why you were so reluctant to talk about him? Or was it because you were still upset about his death?"

Jake shrugged. "A bit of both, I guess. But it was anger, too. Everybody was so damn ready to believe the worst of Bill. I figured if I ever got into a discussion of him, I'd just get so angry that I'd spill the whole thing."

She nodded, suddenly understanding so much as relief flooded her body, just pure blessed relief. The man she thought she had married had not been a dream, but was still at her side. Jake was still a husband she could respect and love. He was dearer to her than ever, now that she knew the truth. Tears came to her eyes.

"If only you had told me earlier," she said quietly.

"I told you, I wasn't supposed to." He swallowed hard. "But I couldn't let you think the things you were thinking. I was too afraid you were going to leave, and you mean more to me than anything else." He put his arm around her and pulled her close.

She wished she could tell him that his fears were unfounded, but she had been coming perilously close to that decision herself. "Things will be easier now," she said.

Jake gave her a strange look, then got to his feet, running his fingers through his hair. "In some ways, yes," he agreed slowly, "but not in every way."

She went over to him. "But now that I know the truth—"

"Now that you know the truth, you'll have to watch every word you say, your every reaction, to make sure that you don't let a hint of the investigation slip. It's not just that you can't let the bad guys know, Kaye— you can't talk to anyone about this. Can you imagine the burden of sharing this secret? I wish I hadn't had to tell you at all."

"I'll be careful," she assured him.

"It's not just a matter of being careful," he pointed out. "Hrljic's starting to suspect that someone's prying into his system. He's got his flunkies watching everyone, looking for some sign."

"Hrljic? Is that why you made me out to be such a gold digger at that party?" She could laugh about it now.

Jake looked slightly sheepish. "I had to show a convincing motive for my greed. An expensive wife was the best I could think of."

"I would have been more convincing if I had been warned," she pointed out. "Next time, I'll really be great. I won't spend half of my time glaring at you, wondering if you've lost your mind."

Jake smiled and shook his head. "That glare was the most convincing part. Everyone thought you were just too bored at our little party." His smile died slightly. "I hated doing that. A lot of those people are decent and honest. You would have liked them, and they would have liked you. There are times the game gets to be a bit too much."

"But now that I know, we can talk about it," Kaye told him. "You're not in it alone anymore."

He nodded. "No, but instead, I've brought you into the danger zone, too. You have to start being suspicious of everyone. You have to start being cautious about where you speak, in case the room is bugged."

"Bugged?" In spite of her relief and optimism, some of his worries were dampening her happiness, and she glanced around their living room warily.

"I think we're safe here, but I'm not sure of our phone."

Her eyes found the telephone. It suddenly looked sinister.

"My family doesn't know the truth, and can't know it."

Kaye remembered Marcia's conviction of Bill's guilt and knew that she would believe the same thing of Jake. The publicity the building fire would generate would be enough to condemn Jake in Marcia's eyes. In the eyes, perhaps, of all his relatives.

She suddenly felt very protective of Jake and angry that his own family would doubt him. He was an honorable man. At heart she had always known that, and that was why she had been so tormented and confused by all the evidence to the contrary. Well, if Marcia said anything to her about Jake, she'd tell that self-righteous—

She stopped and took a deep breath, realizing the trap she had fallen into in her thoughts. It would be just as easy to fall into such a snare in action as well. She put her arms around Jake and laid her head against his chest.

"What will you tell your family about the fire?"

He shrugged. "That it was a tragedy, that I feel sorry for the people. All perfectly true, too. But I can't tell them why I had to do it. I have to resist any temptation to defend or justify myself."

"They'll be hurt."

"They'll survive. And once it's all over, both my name and Bill's will be cleared."

Kaye closed her eyes and listened to the sound of his heartbeat. It was steady and strong, just as their love was. They would make it. Anything that came along, they could handle together. Nothing could ever be as bad as the torment of not knowing, of wondering if the man she loved wasn't who she thought he was. After that, everything else would be simple.

Jake's arms tightened around her, and her hands slid over his back. His body was so powerful and strong, yet she could feel the fire lying in wait just beneath the surface. Waiting for her touch to ignite it.

There was no need for words as she silently unbuttoned his shirt, running her hands over his bare chest. An answering fire was growing in her as she felt his urgency through her fingers.

His mouth came down, locking itself to hers as his hands stripped off her dress. The silken folds fell to the floor around her feet in a whispery hush. His tongue and lips devoured her soul and sent her into a swirling mist of needs and desires.

He unfastened her bra, and then they lowered themselves to the floor, still locked together. She lay on her bare back on the soft throw rug. The cool air made little impression on their feverish skin, as their caresses grew more frenzied and more urgent. Their bodies moved in knowing response to their cravings, as they quickly climbed the peaks of desire, going higher and higher until Kaye could only cling to Jake, dizzy with the powerful urges deep within her.

Their need for each other was fiercer than it had ever been as they sought to seal the bond of their devotion. His revelation and the knowledge of the trials ahead made the fires inside them burn even brighter, consuming everything in their path. There seemed to be no time for gentleness and whispered words of love as their bodies demanded a fulfullment that comprised a need for reassurance and shelter.

He came at her strongly, and she took him in, blazing in a fever of sensations. His skin, his breath, the scent of his nearness, were all a blur, lost in the pulsating union of their passion. They seemed to explode then in a burst much brighter than all the fireworks on the Fourth of July, and then clung together, slowly relaxing and returning from their flight amid the stars.

Kaye's muscles ached as if she had been in a fierce fight, yet there was a wonderful sense of victory, too. She looked up into Jake's eyes, saw them overflowing with love, and she knew they would win.

Their love would warm them through the viciousness and anger they would meet. They'd be together, side by side, united by something even stronger than their marriage vows as they endured the insults, the slights, and the hatred.

He gazed down at her, and she saw a montage of emotions race across his face, but could not really read him. All she knew was that she loved him.

Finally, he said quietly, "It's going to be rough, Kaye."

He rolled to his side and held her, seeming to take strength from her gentleness, her honesty, and her love. "It's going to be real rough."

"Jake, I love you," she whispered. "I couldn't be happy thinking you were a crook, because it meant you weren't the man I fell in love with. But because of your honor and strength, we can make it. I know we can."

7

KAYE WALKED BRISKLY TO THE courthouse and hurried up the stairs to Jake's chambers. She knew it was silly, but she had been worried all morning. The weekend had been wonderful. Relief mingled with pride and a determination to outwit the world, but once they went off to work this morning, it had been a different story. Once Jake was out of her sight, all sorts of frightening possibilities began to run through her mind. What if someone found out the truth? What would they do to him? The whole investigation suddenly seemed so dangerous, and everyone around her seemed menacing.

She was so glad when it was finally lunchtime and she could meet him as they had planned. She'd see for herself that he was safe, and they could have a cozy little meal. She'd even brought the food so they wouldn't have to leave the privacy of his chambers. Privacy was so precious to them now.

Kaye smiled at the security guards and hurried into Jake's office. His court was still in session, but he ought to be calling a recess soon. She hung her coat on the rack and sat down on the leather sofa. Her arms ached to hold him.

In less than ten minutes, she heard the rapping of his gavel, and the stentorian voice of the bailiff announcing that court was adjourned until one o'clock. She glanced at her watch and smiled. That gave them an hour and a half.

The door opened. "Look, Ned. I know what I said, but the prosecution had brought up—" Jake stopped in midsentence as he saw Kaye.

She smiled, suddenly uncertain that her impulse to be early had been wise. "Hi, honey," she said hesitantly.

He smiled back, and the love in his eyes reassured her. "We'll talk later, Ned," he said to the other man.

Ned Schatzen didn't look pleased, but he did leave. As soon as the door closed behind him, Kaye was in Jake's arms.

"I'm sorry if I shouldn't have come here to meet you," she apologized. "But I just couldn't wait to see you." She ran her hands across his back and felt something strange under his robe. "Jake, what's that?"

He pulled away and gave her a look. She didn't understand and stared at him.

"So what's the occasion?" he asked as he walked over to his desk.

"The occasion?" What was wrong with him? "We

Honorable Intentions 99

had planned to have lunch together, remember?"

He shook his head quickly as he unzipped his robe and unbuttoned his shirt. A small microphone was taped to his chest. The wire ran down into his pants.

"Jake?" She had known he must use some sort of bugging device, but it was eerie seeing it on him. A shiver ran down her spine, and she clenched her hands tightly to fight her wave of fear.

Jake's look became a glare. He lifted up his pant leg and she saw a small tape recorder strapped to his leg. He pushed a button and unplugged a wire, then lifted the whole thing out.

"This is a pleasant surprise," he said lightly. "I didn't expect to find you here waiting for me."

"No, I guess not." She frowned at the equipment. It wasn't the tiny, sophisticated equipment she'd seen in movies, and it suddenly seemed so easy to detect.

He put the tape recorder and microphone in a drawer of his desk, locking it carefully. "Where are we eating?"

She found it hard to drag her eyes from the desk. What if his secretary unlocked that drawer sometime when he was gone? "I thought we could stay here," she said hesitantly. "It's very cold out."

"I'm not afraid of the cold."

"No." What if someone had walked into the room while he was taking it off?

Jake was watching her strangely, and she felt driven to make some explanation. "I just thought it would be more private here." She held up the bag of food. "I even stopped at the South Seas Gardens and picked up your favorites."

"Egg rolls?"

She nodded.

"Great. All I need is a walk to work up some appetite."

He went over to the closet and took out his sheepskin coat.

"Jake, with the wind-chill factor, it's three below zero."

"That's okay."

Something wasn't okay. She could tell that much from his actions, but she slipped back into her own coat. She followed Jake from his office carrying the bag with their lunch.

It wasn't until they were outside the building that he put his arm around her shoulders. He drew her close to him and kissed her soundly. It pushed aside some of her doubts, but not all of them.

"Jake, what was wrong?"

He shrugged. "I just get nervous there."

They walked across the street to a small square. The unoccupied benches were out of the wind, and they sat down.

"Do you always wear...that thing?" she asked quietly.

He nodded, looking away.

"It seems so awkward," she said. "I thought you'd wear something smaller and less noticeable. Like on TV."

He laughed. "Just about any TV show has a bigger budget than an FBI investigation."

She did not join in his laughter. "I thought I felt it when I hugged you."

"You probably did." He looked into the bag and

took out the cardboard container on top. "I just try not to hug the prosecutors."

"What if they slap you on the back?"

"Then they'd feel it, too."

He seemed so calm about it that a shiver ran through her body. She knew it was not from the cold.

"But then they'd know."

He sighed and took a bite of an egg roll. "Kaye, I'm careful. I've had to be careful for almost two years now."

She nodded, but was not at ease. "Why did we have to leave? I don't suppose you want me on the tape, but I thought you had turned it off."

"I just felt like getting out of there for a while."

"Oh."

She unpacked the bag. Her worries had not gone away upon seeing him. Now she had more concrete things to worry about. She gave him his Szechwan chicken and began to pick at her sweet and sour pork. "I wouldn't have said anything I shouldn't have before you turned off the tape."

"I know."

"Then why the rush to leave your office?"

He put his plastic fork into his container and sighed. "Kaye, I told you it was going to be rough."

"That's not an answer."

He looked away in silence for a long moment. "I think my office may be bugged," he said finally.

"Your office?" she repeated in a horrified whisper, then gazed about them quickly. No one was near them, and she relaxed slightly. "I thought you were the one doing the bugging."

"I told you on Saturday that there have been rumors of the investigation going around and people are getting scared. They want to know who the other moles are."

"Moles?"

"The ones planted to collect evidence," he explained. "Like me."

"There are others?"

He nodded. "I don't know who or how many—it's safer for us not to know one another—but I do know there are other moles all through the system. Hrljic's getting scared and trying to flush some out."

Kaye was getting frightened and reached over to hold his hand. "Will he be able to?"

Jake just shrugged. "I hope not."

"What if he does?"

He shrugged again and went back to his food.

Kaye suddenly felt a shudder of fear. When Jake had told her of the investigation, she had been so relieved that he was not corrupt that she hadn't really realized all that was involved. Oh, she thought she had, but coming face-to-face with it was very different.

Her Jake was walking around with a tape recorder trying to catch people in incriminating conversations. People who did not want to be caught. People who stood to lose a great deal if they were caught. Jake's position suddenly seemed very dangerous.

"Jake, I'm scared," she whispered.

He looked over at her and smiled sadly. "I'm going to be fine. I make a terrific crook, and everybody who's got to believe that does. Didn't you?"

"I didn't want to."

He squeezed her hand. "Hey, don't worry. You convinced them at the Christmas party that you can spend all the money that I bring in. No one suspects me."

She felt slightly better, knowing that she had helped to allay some suspicions of him. She wished she had known at the time, though. She probably could have been even more useful if she'd been consciously playing her part. "Any time I have to give a repeat performance, just let me know."

"Have you rediscovered your yen for an acting career?" he said lightly. Early in their courtship, Kaye had confided to him her childhood desire to be an actress.

"I just want to help you."

He leaned over and kissed her. "We'll both be doing more acting before this thing is over. Don't try to precipitate the inevitable. Now hurry up and eat. It's freezing out here."

Kaye obediently began to eat, but it was impossible to relax totally. She just prayed that she'd have the strength to give him the support he needed.

Hank Sullivan and Ned Schatzen were waiting for them when they got back to Jake's office. The pleasant intimacy of their lunch vanished, and without any warning, Kaye suddenly found herself thrown back into her gold-digger role.

"It's so nice to see you again, Mrs. Corrigan," Hand said smoothly as he and Ned followed them into Jake's inner office.

Kaye immediately thought of the locked desk drawer, but did not let herself glance toward it. She smiled at the men instead, wishing she were wearing something flashier than a pantsuit and a down coat. Warm they might be, but expensive-looking they weren't. Well, she'd have to capitalize on that, somehow.

"And how are you, Ned?" she said and extended her hand.

Ned took it, but glanced behind her at Jake. "We wanted to see you before your afternoon session began."

"Oh, there's no big rush," Hank assured Ned. "A judge can be a little late. It's not like they're going to start a trial without him."

"I try to discourage that," Jake joked.

"Well, I was just going to leave anyway," Kaye said with a cool smile. She moved over to Jake's side and gave him a quick kiss on the cheek. "I'll see you tonight, darling... in my new mink coat."

Jake squeezed her arm in reassurance. "Bye."

Hank walked with her to the door. "You really don't have to rush away just because we're here, Mrs. Corrigan."

"No, it's all right. Really it is. I got what I came for." She cast a seemingly inadvertent glance at her purse.

He opened the door. "I'm glad to hear he's treating you right."

She waved briefly to Jake and hurried out the door. By the time she reached the safety of the hallway, she was trembling. The only picture in her mind was of

Honorable Intentions 105

Jake as she had last seen him, standing next to his desk. What if they knew about him? What if they found out?

She tried to convince herself that neither Hank nor Ned would go through Jake's drawers. But as she walked slowly down the stairs, she could not relax. The sudden shock of finding the men waiting for him, and her need to play the part Jake had given her, had shaken her. The investigation and all its dangers were becoming very real.

Kaye's worries had not lessened by evening, and she definitely was not in the mood for an office Christmas party. She'd much rather be home with Jake than out drinking with her fellow department managers, but the dinner had been planned for a month. It would be awkward to back out now.

Things had to go on as usual, Jake had told her. Any deviation might be noticed and lead to complications. The last thing she wanted to do was cause trouble for Jake, but it was impossible not to worry about him. And equally impossible to pretend to have a good time away from him, she feared. Well, she *had* once considered a career in acting. This would be a good time to see if she had missed her calling.

Taking a deep breath, Kaye went into the restaurant to meet the others. She was a little late, but Gordon's was not a large place. She shouldn't have any trouble finding them. After checking her coat, she began to look through the building. It was an old mansion filled with small private dining rooms throughout its three stories.

She did not find her fellow managers on the first floor or the second, and was about to go up to the third when she heard a familiar voice. Jacqui's uniquely brassy twang was coming from a dining room behind a flight of stairs that Kaye hadn't even known existed.

She went down the narrow hall. As she got farther from the other rooms, the conversation of her own group became louder and drifted out toward her.

"I mean, you should have heard what she said about our expense sheets for that trip to New York," Jacqui was saying. "She acted all huffy just because I wanted to list a few meals we hadn't actually paid for. You know, things you always list on your expense account. They expect you to list them, for godsake. But Kaye refused to make her sheet tally with mine. She wasn't going to list anything she hadn't actually paid for. Not Miss Goody Two Shoes. It was ridiculous."

Kaye heard murmurs of agreement and sympathy as Jacqui went on, "Then I hear on the tube that her husband, a judge no less, has his grubby little hands out and is just raking in bushels of money."

Kaye stood still, not wanting to hear anymore, but unable to take the few steps that would bring her into the room. She heard titters of laughter.

"Maybe she ought to clean up things at home before she tries to reform the rest of the world." Kaye could not identify the male voice that had spoken.

"I mean, I just about died laughing. Who the hell does she think she is? Playing Lady Virtuous when her husband is nothing more than a crook."

Kaye found herself trembling with rage and hurt. She couldn't bear to have them talk that way about

Honorable Intentions 107

Jake. It wasn't fair that he should have to look so guilty in order to uncover those who were. She wished she could go into the dining room and defend him as he deserved. That was what hurt the most: not being allowed to clear his name.

She fought back a strong inclination to leave. It didn't matter that she had had little appetite when she arrived and none now. For the sake of appearances, she had to attend this dinner. She had to smile and laugh and pretend that nothing was different in her life.

Taking advantage of a pause in the conversation, she went forward, pushing aside the beaded curtain to enter the room. She hoped that her smile appeared natural.

"Sorry I'm late," Kaye apologized, "but I couldn't find you."

"Kaye!" Jacqui gushed. "I'm so glad you made it." She got up and gave her a peck on the cheek. "Merry Christmas, hon."

Although the effort almost killed her, Kaye forced herself to give Jacqui a hug. She would play the game the way Jake wanted her to. "Happy holidays, Jacqui."

Then she made her way around the table exchanging greetings with the others. She forced the memory of their laughter out of her mind and tried to concentrate on her role. If that was the kind of friends they were, she didn't need them anyway. She had Jake, and that was enough.

One of the men got up to help her into her chair. Another asked, "Care for a drink, Madam Future President?"

"A little white wine would be fine."

The waiter took her drink order and then asked if she wanted to see the menu or just order one of the specials.

"The tandoori chicken is absolutely fabulous," Linda put in. "And it's a special today, so the appetizer, vegetable, and dessert are all included."

"That's sounds fine to me," Kaye replied. She had little appetite anyway. Anything that would speed up this farcical celebration would be fine.

By the time the waiter returned with Kaye's Chablis, a silence had descended over the group. Apparently, they had nothing to talk about except her and Jake. Oh, stop being paranoid, Kaye chided herself. She sipped her wine and checked her facial muscles to make sure her smile was still in place.

"Is anyone doing anything special for the holidays?" she asked brightly.

There were a few murmured answers, and by the time the meal arrived, they were back in the swing of shop talk. How much better sales were this year than last year. The problem of getting good help even with the high unemployment rate. Kaye was glad they had such an array of safe topics to fall back on, but she could not forget what she had overheard.

She was relieved when the meal was over and the waiter brought the bill. She didn't even care that he had not given them the separate checks they had asked for. She just wanted to leave.

The others were not pleased, though. "Nuts. How are we going to do this?" Jacqui asked. "It'll take forever to break down the individual items and then give everyone a total. If I get a ticket because my parking meter expires while I'm figuring out this mess, I expect you guys to pay it."

"Us?" Bob was astonished. "Just give it to Kaye. She's the one with connections. She can get it fixed for you."

Kaye felt an instant return of her anger, but kept a smile on her face. People had been making that type of remark ever since she married Jake. It had nothing to do with those accusations on television and in the newspapers. She mustn't read any sinister meanings into Bob's undoubtedly innocent joke.

"Sorry," she said lightly. "Jake's in housing, not traffic court."

"Be cheaper to pay the fine, then." Bob laughed. "If you go through Kaye, you'll have two judges to pay off, not just one."

So much for innocent jokes. Though it hurt unbearably, Kaye forced herself to laugh with the others.

"Actually, I think it would be easier just to divide the total by eight," she said.

"Fine with me," Jacqui said and looked around the table. Everyone else seemed to be in agreement also. "Now the only problem is dividing $138.54 by eight."

"That's a little over seventeen dollars per person, plus about another three-fifty apiece for a tip," Bob said. He grinned. "See? With that talent for money, *I* should have become a judge."

It was harder to keep the smile in place this time, but Kaye did it. Luckily, she could concentrate on getting her wallet out of her purse and did not have to look at anyone for a moment.

"It probably would pay better than Timmerman's, too," Bob added with a laugh as he put a ten and some singles on the table. "Can anyone lend me a five until tomorrow?"

No one leaped at the chance, so Kaye pulled another bill from her wallet. "I can, Bob." She handed it across the table to him.

"Don't ask where it's been," Sue joked.

"I don't even care what nefarious deeds it's covered up," he pointed out. "I'm more worried about the rate of interest I'll be charged for borrowing it. Just remember I'm a poor working man, Kaye."

"I'll try to keep that in mind." She got to her feet and tossed her money on the table. "There's my share," she said. "I'd better be going. It was starting to snow when I arrived, and cabs are going to be scarce."

With a quick good-bye to everyone, she hurried from the room. Her eyes were filled with sudden tears, and she knew she had to get away before she broke down. She'd like nothing better than to lean against the wall for support until she felt stronger, but she didn't want to run the risk of meeting any of the others.

It had taken all the strength she possessed not to leap to Jake's defense as soon as she heard the first disparaging comment, but that strength was gone. All she wanted now was to get home to Jake. Home, where everything was safe and she didn't have to pretend anymore.

8

"I ONLY WANTED to know what I should bring for Christmas dinner, but she acted as though she hadn't even thought that far ahead," Kaye said. She took the steaks off the broiler and put them on their plates, then took the baked potatoes out of the oven.

Jake carried two glasses of wine to the table. "Well, Marcia's never been much of a planner."

"It's less than a week until Christmas. Even Marcia must realize that."

He just shrugged and came back to the stove to put the steaming corn into a serving dish. "So what did she finally assign you?"

"Nothing. She promised to call me back in a day or so." Kaye brought the food over to the table.

Jake pulled out her chair for her, giving her a quick kiss as she sat down. "And I'm sure she will. Stop looking for problems where none exist. Marcia's never been my favorite sister-in-law; just don't let her get to you with her sniping."

He had just sat down himself when the doorbell rang. "What wonderful timing," he muttered, about to get up again.

"No, don't," Kaye said, and rose quickly to her feet. "It's probably some reporters, and they'll only harass us more if they find out you're here."

She hurried into the other room to answer the intercom and was surprised to discover that it was Jake's brother Danny. She waited for him to come up to the second floor, then led him to the kitchen.

"Hi, Dan," Jake said, getting to his feet. "Have a seat. Can you join us?"

Danny shook his head. "Hey, I'm sorry for the lousy timing. I thought you'd have finished dinner by now."

"We tend to eat later than civilized folks." Jake laughed. "What can we do for you?"

Danny seemed hesitant to begin and took great pains to hang his coat over the back of a chair. "It's about Christmas," he finally said.

"I called Marcia today," Kaye remarked.

"Yeah, that's why I'm here."

Marcia had sent Danny all the way to their house to tell her what to bring for dinner? No, Kaye decided, even Marcia was not that neurotic. She felt her stomach tighten and glanced over at Jake. He looked pleased that his brother had dropped in.

Kaye turned back to Danny. "Can I get you a drink or some coffee?" she offered.

Honorable Intentions 113

"No, I really can't stay." He cleared his throat nervously. "So, how have things been?"

"Fine," Kaye said quickly.

Danny looked at Jake uneasily. "Mom said you called her and said some reporters were taking potshots at you, and of course we saw all the stuff in the papers. We were just wondering how you were bearing up."

That familiar gnawing in the pit of Kaye's stomach returned. She reached across the table and found Jake's hand. He squeezed her fingers reassuringly.

"Well, Kaye's right," Jake said. "We've been fine."

Danny nodded.

"How have you been?" Jake added.

"Not too good." Danny seemed relieved at the question. "Not too good at all."

Kaye and Jake exchanged worried glances, and her hold on his hand tightened. Now what?

"It's not really me," Danny hurried to explain. "Hell, we weathered this sort of thing after Bill's death, and I figured we could take it again."

"If it's not you, then who is it?" Jake asked quietly. His grip on Kaye's hand tightened almost painfully, but his voice was calm. "Marcia?"

Danny shrugged uneasily. "Not just her. Megan and Mike and Lucy, too. But they're only thinking of Mom," Danny assured him. "With her heart condition, all this worry can't be good for her. Your picture's forever on TV these days, with all sorts of speculation about what you're involved in. It's bringing back all that stuff with Bill."

"Has she said anything?" Jake asked.

Danny shook his head. "You know Mom. None of her kids could ever do anything wrong."

"You don't sound as if you have the same faith in your family," Jake noted quietly.

There was a tense moment of silence; then Danny laughed. "Hey, nobody's perfect. Is there anybody left who doesn't cheat on their income taxes?"

"I don't," Jake said curtly.

"Oh, right. Sure." Danny coughed and pulled at his collar. "Anyway, the real thing Marcia's worried about is the reporters. She's afraid they'll follow you to our house and camp on our doorstep all day. She talked to Mike and Lucy, and they called Megan down at school, and they all decided I should come see you."

"About what?" Kaye asked angrily. "How can we keep the reporters away?"

Jake looked at her. "I think what Danny is trying to tell us is that we aren't welcome at Mom's on Christmas."

Kaye stared at Jake in astonishment, seeing the hurt in his eyes and feeling the pain with him. She turned slowly to his brother. Surely Jake was wrong. His family wouldn't turn him away on *Christmas*.

But Danny didn't disagree with Jake. He merely looked uncomfortable.

"Danny?" Jake *had* to be wrong.

"It's not that you aren't welcome," he said, shifting in his seat. "We just thought it would be better for Mom if you decided not to come."

"And how do you intend to explain that to her?" Jake asked.

"We hoped you'd call her and make some excuse,"

Danny admitted. "Maybe you could say Kaye's mother invited you?"

Kaye could not keep quiet any longer. It wasn't enough that his family didn't want him present on Christmas, but he had to make the excuses to his mother, too. If only they had been invited to her mother's—but only last week Kaye's mother had informed them she would be taking a Caribbean cruise for the holidays. She jumped to her feet in agitation. "This is ridiculous. Why can't you do your own dirty work?"

"Kaye." Jake's voice was resigned, but she wasn't.

"It *is* ridiculous, Jake. Why should you have to be the one to tell your mother? She'll think you don't want to spend the day with her. Or most likely, that I don't want to." She turned to Danny again, her anger turning to rage. "Why should she think poorly of us just because you haven't got the guts to stand up to a few reporters?"

"Kaye, I don't think this is getting us anywhere," Jake said.

She bit her bottom lip to keep from venting her feelings to the hilt. He was right. How could anything she said undo the hurt that had already been done?

"I think you'd better leave," Jake told his brother quietly.

Danny got his coat and practically fled. The sound of the door closing behind him echoed through the quiet apartment.

"Damn."

Kaye went to Jake and put her arms around him. "I never did like Marcia."

"Oh, don't blame her," he said ironically. "Danny said they had all discussed it. He wouldn't do something like this on his own, or even at Marcia's request. No, my brothers and sister all voted me out."

Kaye blinked back the tears in her eyes and held him tighter. He buried his face in her hair, saying nothing for a long time.

"I guess I never expected this turn of events," he said with a slightly bitter laugh. "I figured they might be shocked about the reports, and even might believe the worst, as they did about Bill, but I never thought they'd excommunicate me from the family." Kaye had never heard such pain in his voice.

They held each other in silence. Kaye's heart was bleeding for Jake. Her own small family had never been particularly close, but she knew how much Jake depended emotionally on the Corrigan clan. He had stood up for Bill, and must have hoped, deep down, that they would stand behind him.

Well, his famliy might have failed him, but she wouldn't. She'd give him all the support and love he needed. They were in this thing together, and she wouldn't let him down.

"We'll have one spectacular Christmas here by ourselves," she promised him. "If I can make a pumpkin pie, I can cook a turkey."

"Isn't that a little elaborate for just the two of us?"

"Nip and Tuck will want some, too," she said lightly, gesturing toward the cats, who were eating the canned tuna she had put in their bowls.

"Right." He pulled away from her and looked down

at the table. She looked down also. Their dinner was cold and unappealing.

"Want me to warm that up?" she offered.

He shrugged. "I'm not too hungry."

"Me neither." She picked up the cold steaks. "Looks as if I'll have a terrific bedtime snack for the cats."

"Do you want some help?"

She shook her head. "No, it'll just take a minute to put this away."

He nodded and went silently into the living room. Through the doorway, she saw him sitting on the sofa, staring vacantly at their small Christmas tree.

Suddenly, she hated Jake's family. How dare they hurt him like this! She dashed away her tears with the back of her hand and shoved the food, still in the serving dishes, into the refrigerator. Then, pasting a determined smile on her face, she picked up their glasses of wine and marched into the living room.

"You know what I've always wanted to do?"

He looked up. The sadness in his eyes almost broke her heart. "What, honey?"

She put their glasses of wine on the table next to her and knelt down before him. "I've always wanted to make love under the Christmas tree," she whispered.

She reached up, put her arms around his neck, and held him close. She rained tiny kisses over his face and neck as her hands slowly unbuttoned his shirt. Then she pushed it off him and rested her head against his bare chest. He put his arms around her, and she closed her eyes.

"I love you," she whispered. She had never meant the words more.

Jake bent down, and she felt his lips brush her hair. "I love you too, honey."

She was silent for a time, enjoying the feel of his skin against her and feeling safe within his embrace. "They love you, too," she said suddenly. "They're doing things all wrong, but they *do* love you."

"Yeah."

She heard the doubt in his voice and opened her eyes. "When it's all over and the truth comes out, they'll feel terrible. It's just that your secret crusade is making things hard for them now."

"So they're running from me."

She sat back on her heels. "Jake, maybe you should tell them the truth."

He shook his head quickly. "I shouldn't even have told you. I can't tell everybody who suspects me."

"It's not just anybody. They're your family. You've always been close."

Jake shook his head slowly. "I can't." He smiled slightly as he reached over to brush a strand of hair back from her face. "Now what was that you said about making love under the Christmas tree? Don't you think you might shock Santa?"

Kaye smiled back. "He's not due for another couple of nights. I think we can chance it."

"I hope you're right," he sighed as he joined her on the floor. The lights of the tree sparkled above his head. "I sure don't want Santa mad at me."

Kaye lay back, taking his hand and pulling him down with her. She caressed his chest and his shoul-

Honorable Intentions

der, letting her hands wander down to his waist, then below that. She could feel his desire growing and made her caresses even more fervent.

Her hands reached up into his thick, curly hair to pull his head down to hers. She touched his lips briefly with gentle, teasing brushes, then held him tightly as her own passion grew. Her tongue darted into his mouth, exploring and tasting, determined to remind him of her love. His arms slid underneath her, as he crushed her closer to him.

She smiled up at him when they parted slightly moments later, their breath coming in ragged gasps. "You see, all you have to do is be nice and I'll tell Santa that you've been very, very good," she said with a smile.

Kaye woke up slowly Christmas morning, stretching silently in the darkened bedroom. The bedside clock said it was just past six. Too early to get up even though she knew she wouldn't go back to sleep. She rolled over to see if Jake was awake yet and found that his side of the bed was empty.

"Jake?"

He came out of the bathroom, already dressed. "Merry Christmas, lazybones." He came over and sat on the edge of the bed, giving her a warmly thorough kiss that did not distract her from the issue at hand.

"Why are you dressed already?" she demanded, her arms still around him. "Are you going somewhere?"

"Just to church."

"Isn't it a little early to get up for the eight o'clock

mass? Come on back to bed with me for another half-hour, and then I'll go with you."

"Actually, I wasn't going to St. Mary's."

She must have looked as confused as she felt, for he went on, "It's an old tradition in our family. Mom and Dad would go to midnight mass in our parish church. Then, early on Christmas morning, Mom would drag us older kids down to St. Patrick's, in the poorer part of the city. She said that it was good for us to see that Christmas didn't mean gifts and candy canes for everybody."

"No, that's not what Christmas is all about, is it?" Kaye said.

"I haven't been to St. Pat's in years, but I feel like going this year."

"Would you mind if I went along?" She didn't want to intrude if it was a private thing.

"No." He shook his head. "In fact, I'd like it very much if you did."

She sprang up from bed. "I don't have time to shower, do I?"

Jake laughed and shook his head. "Just throw on something warm. Never mind your Sunday best—it really is a poor parish, and we don't want to flaunt our affluence."

She tied her hair back in a ponytail, slipped on jeans and chukka boots over thick athletic socks. Then she put on a knitted cap and her ski parka.

They left the apartment and drove through the city in silence. Several inches of new snow had fallen during the night, blanketing the city with its freshness and purity. It was dark, and few people were about, leaving the streets still and peaceful. It almost felt as if they were in church already.

St. Patrick's was a small parish church in a run-down area, but it had been built years ago and had the tall steeple and elaborate stained-glass windows of many of the city's older churches. The outside walls were scarred and graffiti-stained, but the stream of people going inside did not seem to notice. There was an aura of festivity in the air.

Kaye and Jake slipped into a back pew. The inside of the church was as shabby as the neighborhood. The pews were worn, and there were no rich decorations on the altar or shrines as there had been in the church she and Jake had been married in. Instead, colorful banners hung from the wall behind the altar. Many of them looked as if they had been made by the children in the parish school. But she felt welcome here, and she remembered the humble birth of Him whose birthday they were celebrating.

Even at this early hour, there was quite a crowd in church. Kaye was especially surprised to see the number of children who accompanied their parents. At least half of them had no boots, just regular street shoes. She was sure that their feet were cold, but their faces just looked excited as they joined in the singing of the traditional carols. It was Christmas and a time to be happy. She reached over and squeezed Jake's hand as the mass started. They were very lucky in so many ways.

The words of the Roman Catholic service were warm and comforting and not so different from the High Episcopalian liturgy she had grown up with that she felt alien. On the contrary, somehow in this humble parish church, she felt closer to the true meaning of Christmas than she ever had before. And with Jake at her side, she felt strong. All *would* be well. His name would be cleared eventually, and his family would be just as proud of him as she was. In the meantime, they had each other and their love, and were bound to all who suffered anxiety, no matter what one reason...

The ride home was just as silent as the ride to St. Patrick's. It was light now, and more people were out, but there seemed to be a stillness in the air that they hesitated to break.

"Your mother was very wise to take you to St. Pat's," Kaye murmured to Jake as they drove back to their apartment. Jake made French toast while Kaye set the table with the special Christmas china his mother had given them as a wedding gift. They only had two place settings, but Mrs. Corrigan had promised them more when they needed it. Kaye smiled as she folded a napkin. Mrs. Corrigan was not very subtle about wanting more grandchildren.

After breakfast, they opened their presents. Along with the usual clothing and tapes for the stereo, Kaye had given Jake a cashmere sports jacket and a science-fiction trilogy. She also had put together a scrapbook with pictures of Jake and Bill that she'd found in a drawer of Jake's desk. He seemed especially moved by it.

He had bought her a camera she had been wanting plus extra lenses and equipment, and some paperback mysteries she had not read yet. But the best present was a gigantic teddy bear that was almost as tall as she was. It held a sign that said she was bearing up well.

"It'll also keep you company in case they send me to jail," he joked.

Safe in the intimacy of their own home, she was able to laugh.

Late in the morning, Jake called his mother. He and Kaye had decided to use Danny's lie and tell his mother that they were spending Christmas with Kaye's mother in California. Jake hated practicing such subterfuge on his mother, but it would hurt her less than the truth.

"Merry Christmas, Mom," he said cheerfully when she answered her phone.

"Merry Christmas to you, too, Jake."

"Just wanted you to know our flight was fine, Mom."

"I heard it was in the seventies out there in L.A. Must be hard to take."

"Yeah, right, Mom." He turned away from the window that overlooked the snow-covered street. "Too bad we won't be here long enough to get a tan."

"Maybe you should take a few more days off. It'd do you good to get away a little longer and get some rest."

That was his mother, always worrying about him. "I wish I could, but I'm afraid my tan will have to wait."

"You sound just like your father." She snorted. "Work always came first, and did anybody care? No. And they won't with you, either. Hard work just doesn't seem to be rewarded anymore. All you get is another fool reporter trying to make his career by ruining yours."

She stopped talking when he laughed. "If I ever run for office, I think I'll make you my campaign manager."

"Go ahead and laugh," she said. "But I'll tell you something. As much as I miss not having you here with us for Christmas, I'm glad you were able to get away. It's better for both you and Kaye. More peaceful."

Jake didn't know what to say, but his anger toward his family returned. Why had they put him in this position?

"Well, this is costing you a fortune, son. Give Kaye a kiss for me and tell her mother I hope she's having a nice holiday. I'll see you when you get back."

Jake hung up the phone softly and stared out the window. Even though they had not left the city, he and Kaye were having the peaceful Christmas his mother had wanted him to have. He would hate to see it end and wondered if there wasn't some way to make it last a few more days.

He found Kaye in the kitchen, staring down at a recipe. He put his arms around her, hugging her tightly to him as he kissed her neck.

"What do you say we take a mini-vacation? Maybe go up to Wisconsin for some skiing?"

She turned in his arms to face him. "Could we? It

would be so wonderful to get away for a while. Could we go soon, or would it be too hard to get reservations so close to New Year's?"

"I'll find us a place some way, even if I have to beg, borrow, or steal."

"Jake, that's not funny."

He kissed her forehead tenderly. "How about if I just agree to pay double?"

"That's okay."

Kaye yawned comfortably and hugged Jake a little closer to her. She knew Jake missed his family, but it had actually been a very pleasant holiday. Things had been so hectic lately that it was a luxury for just the two of them to spend a day alone. They had fixed dinner together. Then, after cleaning up, they snuggled up on the couch by the bay window as Jake went through her scrapbook, telling her about Bill.

The two brothers had been very close as they grew up, even though Bill had been four years older. Bill taught Jake to play baseball and football, and during the summers, they swam together and rode their bikes all over the city. The city and the way it worked had fascinated Bill, and he had passed that love on to Jake. It wasn't a fascination with politics, but with the people and how the city should serve them. And that's what Bill had done right up until the time his car swerved on an icy patch of road and slid into the path of the truck.

They sat in silence for a long time after Jake closed the scrapbook and laid his head in her lap. Kaye felt closer to him than she ever had before, because she could see so much of what had shaped him. Bill had always been the mystery in his life. The influence that he never would talk about. She was very moved that he finally had.

She glanced over at Jake and smiled when she saw that he had fallen asleep. Then she turned to stare out the window at the steadily falling snow. It looked so beautiful and peaceful as it clung to the bare branches of the trees. The normal sounds of the street were muffled, and she felt slightly drowsy herself.

Jake stirred in his sleep. He was lying with his head in her lap, and she smiled fondly down at him. Some of his hair had fallen across his forehead, and he looked like a little boy. She wondered idly what it would be like to have a little Jake nursing at her breasts.

She brushed his hair back lightly, careful not to disturb him. The thought of children had been floating into her mind more and more lately. When this whole undercover business was over, she and Jake would have to talk about it.

She turned to stare out the window again, wondering just how long that would be.

9

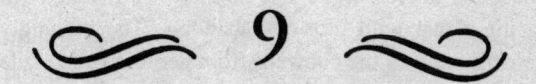

"I CAN'T BELIEVE you actually managed this," Kaye said as they pulled up to the inn. "Three whole days of peaceful anonymity." Just the idea of it made her feel lighthearted and relaxed.

Jake glanced around at the ski resort. "I just wish I could have gotten us a room at Telemark. Their slopes are a lot better than these."

"This is great. Stop fussing," she sighed. "Plus it's a lot closer to Chicago. We won't have to leave until late on New Year's Day. That gives us more time to relax." She leaned over to kiss his lips gently. "And I don't mean on the slopes."

"It sounds as if you have designs on my virtue," he teased her, and got out of the car. He went around to her side and helped her out. "I think I should warn you that I'm a married man and don't fool around."

"So who's fooling?" She sidled up close to him and put her arm around his waist. "I want you to know that I'm quite serious about this."

He smiled down at her, his eyes reflecting his love. "So am I, sweetheart. So am I."

They checked into their room, and since there was still time before dinner, they went out to the slopes. Kaye was not an expert skier, but the runs at Alpine Valley presented no problem to her. She and Jake had chosen a fairly simple one to start with, and went racing down with glorious abandon. The bracingly cold air blew all the cobwebs from her mind and made her skin glow.

They moved up to a slope that was slightly more difficult but considerably less crowded. Gliding along on the glistening surface of the snow seemed to renew her spirit, and she hated to stop, even when Jake complained that he was starving. She cajoled him into one last run down the slope; then they took their skis off and carried them back toward the inn.

"I feel marvelous," Kaye said. "I had forgotten how much fun this was."

"I'm glad the fact that I'm starving to death didn't hamper your enjoyment," Jake grumbled.

She punched him playfully, then raced him up to their room. He won easily.

"It's these boots," she pointed out. "They're no good for running."

"They're the same as mine." He stripped off his down vest and the thick sweater he wore beneath it. "You're just a poor loser."

Honorable Intentions 129

She pretended to pout as she undressed, but was glad to see him returning to his normal lighthearted teasing. Christmas had been a strain on him. Getting away was the best possible thing for both of them. She pulled off her own sweater and saw that Jake was standing by the dresser, staring down at the newspaper the maid had left. Tension had returned to the air.

"Losers get the bathroom first," she called out.

He turned around abruptly. "Who says?"

"Me." She grinned as she stood up. "Besides, you aren't ready for a shower." She nodded toward his jeans.

"I can be ready in a second," he informed her as he unzipped his pants. "But since I'm a better winner than you are loser, I'm willing to share the bathroom with you."

"How kind, O Gracious One," she mocked, following him into the tiny bathroom. Her eyes were on the firm muscles of his buttocks and legs. Her hands itched to stroke them.

"You're going to have to repay me for this honor," he told her.

"Oh?" She tore her eyes away from him and brushed her hair briskly. She twisted it into a coil and pinned that to the top of her head. "Do you mean I have to find you a fleet of tiny boats to play with, or just wash your back?"

He reached into the shower and turned on the water, testing it with his hand until it reached the right temperature.

"I've given up playing with toys in the bathtub, and I can think of better things for you to wash than my back." He pulled aside the shower curtain for her to enter.

"I'm not sure my mother would approve," she said as she went into the warm spray.

Kaye ran a bar of soap over Jake's damp chest, working her fingers over his hair-roughened skin until there was a good lather. Then she spread it around, across his chest and over his shoulders. Her hands slid under his arms, down his sides, and back around his waist.

"This is certainly a big job," she murmured and lathered him with the soap again.

"Are you saying that I'm fat?"

"Just husky," she said with a smile.

In order to reach his back, she had to press her body close to his and wrap her arms around him. She wiggled slightly against him, enjoying the contact of flesh to flesh.

"I could turn around," he offered.

"And risk slipping on this tile? No, that's all right. We slaves are adaptable."

She moved even closer to him, her body pressing against his soap-slippery skin. Running her hands over his back and down over his butt, she could feel the muscles move under her touch. Her own body grew warm in response, and the movement of her hands slowed into rhythmic caresses. She could feel his desire against her, and she raised her mouth for his kiss. His tongue probed and prodded in sensuous delight.

"The slave is slowing slightly," he pointed out with a tender smile and took the soap from her.

He rubbed it over her skin, moving quickly, over

her back and around to her flat stomach. His hands cupped her breasts, the roughness of his fingers making the tips harden with longing. Then his caress moved on. Down the sides of her legs and finally in between her thighs. Desire began to race through her being, surging forward as on the crest of a wave.

"This is the nicest shower I've had in a long time," she murmured, wrapping her arms tightly around him.

Jake managed to get the soap back in the dish before his embrace engulfed her. His mouth came down on hers, demanding yet gentle, as his tongue explored hers. Its thrusting and probing seemed to echo the rapid beat of her heart. She clung to him, only vaguely aware of the water rushing down at her.

He pulled back suddenly. "I think it's time we adjourned to another room."

She looked faintly puzzled, then reached to turn off the water. Jake got out of the shower first and held out a large white towel. She stepped into it, and he rubbed her briskly, drying her skin and at the same time increasing the heat in her blood.

When she was dry, she performed the same service for him, rubbing, drying, and caressing with the big fluffy towels until they both were breathing more rapidly. Then they went back into the bedroom, neither of them speaking as they fell into each other's arms on the bed. They had loved each other long enough to know the other's rhythm. Their caresses heightened their desires; their touch bonded them together, pledging once again their love.

When they finally made it to the dining room sometime later, Kaye felt bathed in happiness. A contented glow seemed to surround her, including Jake in her world of peace and joy. They sat at their table wrapped only in each other's presence. The waiter intruded every now and then to bring their food, but never enough to break the spell.

"It's him. I know it's him."

During the main course of their meal Kaye began to notice some disturbance around them. At first, she tried to ignore it and pretend it wasn't happening, but the harder she tried to hold on to their fragile shell, the faster it seemed to slip away.

"It's got to be that judge. I recognize him from all the pictures."

Kaye glanced around them. A group at a nearby table was watching them avidly.

"Just ignore them and eat," Jake said in a low voice.

She turned back to her steak, but her appetite was gone, and the meat tasted like cardboard. Forcing herself to take a few more bites, she felt herself straining to hear the whispered conversation from the other table even though she didn't really want to know what they were saying.

Suddenly, there was someone next to their table. She looked up to see one of the men from the neighboring table. She suspected he had had too much to drink.

"You're John Corrigan, aren't you? The judge who's letting people burn? How many little kids did you hurt to pay for this ski trip?"

Jake was on his feet in an instant. He was angry and trying not to explode. She wasn't sure he would win his battle and got to her feet also, reaching her hand out toward him.

"Jake," she said quietly.

He looked at her, reading the plea in her eyes. What good would a fight do? It would only call more attention to them, and they didn't need that. One of the other diners led the man away and back to his own table.

"Let's just go, Jake."

He nodded and led her from the dining room. "I guess I should have expected this," he sighed once they were alone. "Most of the people here are from the city. Telemark would have been a better spot."

"It's not that far away," she pointed out, feeling as though all eyes were on them as they left the dining room. Their magic spell of happiness had been broken.

They spent the next morning on the slopes, and then, after a hot lunch, they rented cross-country skis and followed a pleasantly scenic trail through the woods. While they were alone with each other, they relaxed and their happiness soared, but as they neared the inn in the late afternoon, Kaye felt herself growing tense.

"I don't really feel like dressing up tonight. Why don't we order up a dinner from room service?" she suggested once they were back in their room.

Jake was not fooled by her excuse. "Are you letting them chase you away?"

"No, I'm trying to keep them from spoiling our day, that's all," she said. "What's so great about being brave and stoic and appearing in the dining room each night if it's going to ruin my appetite and make me upset?"

He put his arm around her shoulders. "You're right. I just hate to let them know they've gotten to me. I'm so damn stubborn I'd sit there all night rather than let anyone drive me away."

She felt torn. "Maybe that's the way it ought to be. You haven't done anything wrong. Why shouldn't we eat in the dining room?"

"Because it bothers you when people recognize me," Jake said. "That's reason enough."

In the end, they did go to the dining room. Kaye was afraid that hiding in their room would only make it look as if Jake were guilty of something. They asked for a more secluded table near the windows and had a relatively undisturbed meal. Kaye forced herself to eat even though she felt as if everyone in the room was watching them. She did not fool Jake, though. He sensed her tension and was upset.

"This vacation isn't working out as I had planned," he said.

"It's fine. I'm having a good time," she insisted. "I'll get used to the attention."

"You shouldn't have to," she snapped. "I should never have involved you in any of this."

Kaye knew he was angry with himself, not her, but even so, his words hurt. The little appetite she had had vanished.

"I love you," she whispered. "If you're involved, then *I* want to be."

He threw his napkin down on the table. "I didn't

give you much choice in the matter, did I? For someone who professed to love you so much, I was pretty damn selfish."

"Jake, don't." She reached across the table for his hand. "This kind of talk hurts more than the attention and the rumors."

He forced a smile. "I'm sorry. I guess we should have stayed in our room to eat. Who cares what they think? The whole world is sure I'm guilty anyway, so we may as well please ourselves. This trip was supposed to relax us, so let's start letting it."

They stayed very much to themselves for the rest of the time at the ski resort. They had to share the slopes with other skiers, certainly, but they never stayed in one place long enough to be bothered by anyone. By the time they went home, they had learned to insulate themselves from the rest of the world. Or so Kaye thought.

THE CORRIGANS: THE STORY OF CORRUPTION IN THE COURTS.

Kaye stood in her office and stared at the newspaper in her hands. She could not believe the headlines. For the next week, the newspaper ran a continuing story about Jake, Bill, and even their father, who hadn't been involved in any of this; he had died more than ten years ago. Yet the tabloids hinted that he, too, had been corrupt—only there had been no proof of his wrongdoing.

She read the first few paragraphs filled with insinuations and felt sick, aching for Jake's mother and how much this all must hurt her. How much longer would it go on?

"Kaye." Her assistant manager poked her head into Kaye's office. "Security just threw out another reporter, and they're getting tired of it. They want to know if you can work upstairs in the main offices today."

How could she do that? All her papers were here. "Has it really been that bad out there?"

The other woman shrugged with a wry smile. "Well, outside of the phone ringing constantly with some reporter wanting to talk to you and those actually coming up here to find you, it's been real quiet. I even had time to wait on a customer."

Kaye sighed. "I guess I'd better go up there, then, although I'm not sure what good it will do."

She packed up her things and carried them up to a small conference room in the executive office suite. There was a phone there, but she felt as if she were imprisoned. Her tension increased when she wasn't even allowed to go down to the cafeteria for lunch. A rather ungracious secretary brought her a salad and some lukewarm coffee.

She spent a good part of the afternoon pacing back and forth in the small room. She had projections to work on and the past quarter's sales figures, but the closeness of the room was getting to her. It was ridiculous, she knew, for her office downstairs was even smaller, but she was feeling claustrophobic. Just the knowledge that she wasn't supposed to leave the office suite had her climbing the walls. She finally decided

Honorable Intentions 137

to leave a little early and slipped down to the loading dock where she called a cab.

A few people seemed to resent the trouble caused by the reporters, but not very many. It was just being shoved about as she had been, unable to work in her own office where she preferred to be, that had upset her so. After all, the store had real business to attend to, and she couldn't blame them for wanting her out of the way. They didn't want the customers annoyed by reporters. But no matter how she tried to reason with herself, she still had a splitting headache.

Once she was settled into the cab, she leaned back and closed her eyes. It would be good to get home. She would take a nice hot bath and fix something simple for dinner. Or maybe they'd order a pizza. That would be even better. She could just relax for once...

The cab pulled to a stop. "Three seventy-five, lady."

Kaye opened her eyes with a start. Boy, she was really tired and starting to fade fast. A bath and a good strong cup of coffee would perk her up.

"Keep the change," she told the driver and handed him a five-dollar bill. She climbed out of the cab and slammed the door. It was only when she was standing on the sidewalk that she saw the people in front of her house.

"Mrs. Corrigan?"

They rushed toward her, cameras flashing and voices shouting. The blinding light hit her right in the eyes, and she felt rather than saw the microphones that were pushed into her face. After the way they had been hounding her at the store, she should have expected them to be here also, but she hadn't. Home was supposed to be safe and peaceful.

"Mrs. Corrigan, do you have any comment about your husband's pending indictment?"

"No." She tried to push through them, but there were so many. They kept closing in around her, and she began to grow frightened.

"Were you aware that he was soliciting and accepting bribes?"

"Please, let me by." She held up her hand to shield her face from the bright light. The reporters seemed like vultures waiting for their prey.

"Where is your husband now?"

"Is it true that you've initiated divorce proceedings against your husband?"

My God! Had they no mercy? "No, I have not," she cried angrily. "Now get out of my way."

She could feel the hot tears of rage flow down her cheeks, but did not care. This was her home, and she was not going to let them peck at her until she bled. With a strength that she didn't know she possessed, she pushed her way through the crowd. The reporters followed, shouting questions and shoving microphones in her face, but she ignored them.

Somehow she managed to get inside the house and slam the entry door behind her; then she ran up the stairs to the apartment. Her hands were shaking, and she could hardly fit the key into the lock. Finally, the door opened, and she practically fell inside. The dark silence of the apartment seemed safe and welcoming.

She sat at their dining room table for a long time, not even bothering to take her coat off. She was exhausted and could barely stop shaking. After a while, she went into the kitchen and poured herself a bourbon and water. It took half the drink before her trembling was under control. Then she carried the glass into the darkened living room and sank into the sofa.

The drapes were open, and she could see the lights of the city outside. She knew she ought to close the curtains and turn on the lights, but she was afraid to. The TV crews were probably still out there with some kind of telescopic lens that would let them look right into her home. It seemed so much safer here in the dark where they could not see her. She pulled her coat closer around her, wishing Jake would get home.

Jake! How would he get past the reporters? It would be even worse for him than for her. He was the one they wanted to interview, to push and prod forever.

She hurried to the telephone. Using only the light from the dial, she called his chambers. There was no answer. She glanced at her watch. Maybe he'd be at the Civic Center. She called, but no one there had seen him. They suggested she call party headquarters.

Her mouth dry with fear, Kaye took a gulp of her drink and dialed the number. The phone rang and rang at party headquarters, but no one answered. If only she could warn him, he could sneak around to the back door. Her hands started to shake again at the thought of her husband having to sneak into his own home. It wasn't fair.

A sudden noise at the front door made her jump. Lord, how did they get inside? There was the sound of a key in the lock.

They couldn't do this. They couldn't just break

into the house. She reached for the phone again and pushed the bottom button. "Operator, get me the police."

The door opened, and the room was suddenly flooded with light. It was Jake.

"Hi, honey." His smile faded as a puzzled frown took its place. "When'd you get home?"

"How did you get in?" she asked hoarsely. Her hands were still shaking. How could he come in smiling? Had the reporters disappeared? She put the phone back down.

Jake appeared not to have heard her. "Why were the lights off? Why are you still wearing your coat? Did you just get in?"

"I asked you first. How did you get in?" Her voice rose to a shrill pitch.

He frowned. "Through the door, why?"

"Which door?" she snapped impatiently.

"The front door."

"The front door!" she cried, her voice climbing even higher. "How did you get past that mob of TV people?"

"The same way you did," he replied with a casual shrug. "A buddy warned me the reporters were here, so I just asked the district to give us an escort home. They sent a couple of patrol cars along."

Kaye's voice deserted her as he went on, a smile on his face. "I just slipped them a few 'no comments,' and zipped right in."

For some reason, she was blazing angry, and his easy smile fueled her rage. "A few 'no comments' and you zipped right in?" she screamed. "I had to fight my way in. Then I was worried sick when I couldn't find you."

She paused to take a breath. "Then you get a police escort home. It must be nice to be an almighty judge. It's too bad a plain little taxpayer can't get the same kind of service."

She felt wrenching sobs coming and ran into the bedroom. She threw herself on the bed, crying loudly into her pillow.

Somewhere in a fog, she heard a worried voice. "Kaye?"

Jake shook her shoulder lightly, and she turned over. Through her tears, she saw Jake sitting on the edge of the bed. "What do you want?" she said raggedly.

"Kaye, I had them send a car over to the store to escort you home. Didn't they bring you?"

She shook her head. "I left early and called a cab." She felt stupid for reacting hysterically, but she didn't seem able to stop the tears.

"Want me to help you with your coat?"

She nodded, sitting up and he eased it off her, then helped her out of her long-sleeve dress. It was cool with just her slip on, but she didn't have the energy to put on her robe. She just lay face down on the bed again.

She had certainly been wrong. She had thought that no matter what happened, their love would be a safe and secure place for them to retreat to. A place that the rest of the world could not touch. But today had proved her wrong. If the pressures could upset her enough to make her angry at Jake, nothing was safe. There was no place they could retreat to.

Strong but gentle fingers began moving over her body. They crushed the exhaustion in her shoulder and neck muscles, forcing the tension down her body and finally pushing the weariness into her feet. From there all the pain and irritability was squeezed out of her toes. A comfortable tiredness was left.

"Jake?"

"Hmmm?"

"Will it be over soon?"

His hands stopped moving, and she heard him sigh. "I hope so, honey. Lord, I hope so."

10

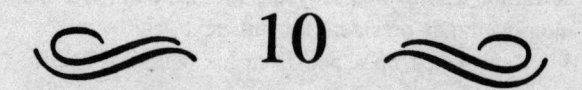

KAYE FOUND A message stuck on her phone when she walked into her office, and read it as she took off her coat. Matt wanted to see her as soon as she came in. Kaye wasn't surprised. It was probably about those reporters who had been in the store last week.

Jake had promised that the press wouldn't bother her anymore, and they hadn't. She didn't know how he had done it, but she could assure Matt that the incident would not be repeated.

She took off her boots and slipped into her shoes, then hurried up to Matt's office. He was waiting for her.

"Good morning, Kaye." Matt looked tired, Kaye thought as she sat down.

"If it's about those reporters," Kaye began. "You don't have to worry—"

He put up his hand as he shook his head. "No, it's

not the reporters. Well, not exactly."

Kaye stopped speaking and waited. There was an awkward moment of silence while Matt seemed to search for the right words. Kaye felt a twinge of concern in the pit of her stomach. Matt had never had problems talking to her before. They had always gotten along very well. In fact, Matt was the one who had suggested that Kaye serve on the merchants' association during the past year, and that had led to her nomination as president for this next year.

Matt picked up a pen from his desk and fiddled with it. "I got a call yesterday concerning you," he said, and looked up. "The Greater Avenue Merchants' Association would like you to withdraw your name from the ballot."

Kaye was stunned. "But the nominating committee approved me."

"Yes, they did, but since next year's slate of officers was put together, you've gained a certain notoriety. The kind the association would rather not have its president involved in."

Kaye just stared at him. "They don't want me to be president because of Jake?"

Matt looked slightly uncomfortable. "Not Jake, exactly," he hedged. "It's the attention he's getting and the rumors that are going around."

"But they aren't true."

He shrugged impatiently. "Look, Kaye, I don't like this any better than you do, but there's nothing either of us can do about it."

Kaye was angry and in no mood to slip silently away as Matt seemed to be hoping she would. She had worked hard for the merchants' association this past year and would do a good job as president. It wasn't fair that the nominating committee should forget all of her qualifications and zero in on Jake's problems. They had nothing to do with how she would handle the position. She would like the chance to point that out to them.

"Why isn't there anything we can do? Why can't we fight their decision?" Kaye asked. "I could refuse to turn in my resignation."

Matt leaned back in his chair with a sigh. "What good would that do, Kaye? The merchants' association isn't a battleground to prove anyone's innocence. It's an organization of business people who are trying to solve some common problems. Your nomination as president would only distract them from solving those problems. And distract public attention from the real accomplishments that have been made."

Kaye looked away. She was just beginning to feel the pain and disappointment. "So you're on their side."

"It's not a matter of sides," Matt pointed out. "I'm trying to do what's best for everyone. Both you and the association."

Kaye said nothing. She was numb.

Matt's tone was softer, as if he understood Kaye's feelings, when he continued, "It's true that you don't have to withdraw, Kaye. There is no way that they can force you to, but if you don't, you run the risk of facing an opposition candidate and losing the election. That would be a first in the history of the association, and very embarrassing to the nominating commmittee."

"How unfortunate for them," Kaye replied sarcastically.

"Kaye, look at it from their point of view. Your nomination is very controversial right now, and they don't like controversy."

Kaye took a deep breath and let it out slowly. The hurt was still there, but some of her anger was fading. "I wanted that job."

"I know," Matt said quietly. "And maybe you can get it next year or the year after. But it's not the right time for you now. You already had problems with reporters last week, and if your nomination is publicly announced, it will draw the media to you even more. If you withdraw now, everything can be swept under the rug. That's best for you and for Jake."

Kaye did see the truth in what Matt said even though it hurt to admit it. She didn't think she could face all those reporters again. She sighed, feeling defeated. "I'll work up a letter."

"I've already got one prepared," Matt said. "Would you like to review it?"

Kaye hesitated, annoyed that the merchants' association had been so certain she'd obey orders that they even had her letter written for her. Was she really that much of a puppet? They pulled the strings and she danced. Or rather signed letters.

"No, I don't need to see it." She didn't care if her voice sounded bitter.

"It's rather innocuous," Matt said. "Increased work load. That kind of thing."

"I'm sure it's fine."

Honorable Intentions

Matt pushed a paper across the desk toward her. "You will have to sign it."

Kaye nodded and quickly scrawled her signature without reading the letter. Matt put it aside and stood up.

"I really am sorry, Kaye. Believe me, we know you're doing a good job here at Timmermen's and there's no question about your position..."

There was no way that Kaye could speak. She just nodded and left Matt's office before she broke down. Would the investigation creep into every part of their lives? Was nothing safe from it?

"I don't think it's too bad," Jake said a few days later after he finished the last forkful of beef stew on his plate. "Could use a little more pepper to suit my taste."

"It tastes fine to me," Kaye said listlessly.

He looked across the kitchen table at her, trying to hide his concern. She had been awfully quiet for the last few days. Every time he asked her if something was wrong, she insisted she was fine, but he knew that she was hiding something. It was hard not to press her and insist that she tell him what was the matter, but he was determined not to. She had a right to her own space. When she wanted to talk, she would.

"I got the recipe out of that *Dinner in Thirty Minutes* cookbook you gave me for my birthday," he told her.

She nodded, barely looking up. Her plate was still two-thirds full.

He went on doggedly. "If this stew is any example, that cookbook should get a lot of use. I made this in twenty-eight minutes flat."

"That's good."

Her expression didn't change, and she avoided his penetrating gaze.

"The tossed salad took me another eight minutes, though. Do you think that counts?"

"I don't know."

He wondered if the reporters had been bothering her again. He would have expected her to mention it if they had, but she hadn't said anything. Was she trying to be brave? He watched for a moment as she pushed the food around on her plate.

"You don't have to finish if you don't want to." Then, attempting to insert some levity, he added, "But you can't have any dessert."

"I'm not that hungry," she replied, apparently missing the joke as she stood up from the table.

Maybe she was just tired or coming down with a cold and needed some rest. "I'll clean up, hon. There isn't that much."

"That's all right."

"No, really," Jake said. "It's no big deal. And I thought you had a meeting tonight. Or is it next Thursday?"

She picked up her dishes without looking at him. "I don't have any meetings coming up at all."

He got his plate and silverware and followed her over to the sink. "Sure you do." How could she have forgotten something so important to her? "The merchants' association. Doesn't it always meet on Thursdays? Or don't you have to attend now that you're going to be president?"

"I quit." She began to run the water and rinse the dishes.

"You what?" He reached over and turned off the faucet. "What do you mean you quit?"

"Just what I said." She was beginning to sound a bit irritated. "I decided I didn't want to do it anymore, and I quit."

She turned back to the sink and finished rinsing off the dishes. Jake just stared at her, his anger growing rapidly.

"You didn't quit. You really wanted that job."

"I changed my mind."

"Why?" he challenged her.

She had begun to load the dishwasher, but she straightened up, glaring at him in real annoyance. He didn't care. He wanted to know if this was all because of the investigation, as he feared.

"I was tired of all the meetings and the stupid bickering over every idea. I'd rather spend the time with you." She began to load the dishes again.

"I don't believe you." An awful fear was growing in him. "I don't believe you changed your mind at all."

She looked up at him, her eyes sad and tired. "Leave it, Jake. Just leave it."

"No." His fear was augmenting itself with great rapidity. "Why did you quit?"

She carried the casserole over to the sink. "I was asked to," she said quietly.

"Because of me." It wasn't a question.

"I've gained a certain notoriety lately that the association doesn't approve of, to quote Matt." She ran the water into the sink, not looking at him.

"Didn't he mean your husband had gained it, not you?" Jake asked bitterly.

Kaye shrugged her shoulders. "I guess."

"What did they do, just throw you out?"

"Oh, no, they were very civilized about it. They asked me to turn in my resignation."

"Why didn't you refuse?" Jake cried, his anger bursting out, surprising both himself and Kaye. "Dammit, you haven't done anything wrong."

"Neither have you."

He didn't understand how she could sound so reasonable about the whole thing. Why wasn't she angry? God knew, he was furious.

"Why didn't you throw the resignation back in their faces and let the members decide whether or not they wanted you as president?"

"I thought of it," she admitted with a tight little smile. "And I was very tempted, but Matt talked me out of it."

"I'll bet he did," he said shortly. "I can imagine how he'd feel about you disregarding their royal command."

"No, it wasn't that," she argued. "He just didn't think I'd gain anything by fighting them. Even if I won the election, there'd be a lot of hard feelings and bad publicity. I don't think I could take all those reporters again."

He remembered all too clearly how the reporters had upset her. Just another way he had helped her to

Honorable Intentions 151

lose her innocence since they were married. What would he do to her next?

"Kaye, I'm sorry." The apology seemed so inadequate. And so repetitive. "That's getting to be my favorite phrase, isn't it? I'm surprised that you're still around to hear it."

"Jake, don't." She came over and took his hand when he tired to turn away from her. "We're in this together. Things will work out."

"Will they?" A sudden thought came to him. "When did Matt tell you? Is this what you've been upset about for the last few days?"

"He told me Tuesday morning."

"Three days ago. Why did you wait so long to tell me? Or weren't you going to tell me?" He felt even more hurt that she hadn't confided in him right away.

"What was the point? I knew you'd just get angry and blame yourself, just as you're doing. How is that going to help anything?"

Jake felt sick. He was causing problems for his family and was wreaking havoc with Kaye's professional life. He turned and went into the living room to stand at the front window and stare down at the street. He didn't see anything but the hurt in Kaye's eyes.

Kaye came up behind him. "Do you want to wrestle a little?"

He just shook his head.

"Why not? Afraid I'll win?" She ran her fingers through the hair on the back of his neck.

"No chance of that," he mumbled, with pretended male chauvinism.

She put her arm around his waist and leaned her head against his back. "Jake, you must really think quite highly of yourself to imagine that you're the cause of all my problems."

"I can't joke anymore, Kaye. Every damn time we turn around, my involvement in this project gets you a kick in the head. It's not fair that your life should be destroyed by this."

"I do have a few problems because of your activities, Jake. But I can manage. Gladly."

He opened his mouth to speak, but Kaye went right on.

"I mean it, Jake. You're helping to clean things up. To get back the kind of system of justice we ought to have."

He still would not look at her. "It's hurting you," he insisted stubbornly. "You're tougher than I ever thought, but I know it's hurting you. When it's all over, you'll have lost every vestige of innocence."

"We'll both be different when it's over, Jake," she said softly, and moved around in front of him to look into his face. "There's no way we can prevent that, but we can be proud of what we've done, too."

He just held her close.

The telephone awoke Kaye from a sound sleep. As she reached for the receiver, she was surprised to see that the time was just past eleven. It felt later, like the middle of the night.

"Hello," she mumbled sleepily.

"Gimme Jake," the voice commanded.

Honorable Intentions — 153

She was surprised at the brusque greeting, but just tapped Jake on the shoulder with the phone.

He took it from her. "Jake Corrigan."

He didn't say another word, but Kaye was alert suddenly, feeling his growing tension. Sleep was far away.

"Yeah, I know the place," he said, and then was silent a moment longer. "Give me an hour."

The caller must not have liked that, because Jake protested in turn. "Look, I have to wake up first. I'm not going to do you any good if some patrolman has to scrape me off a telephone pole."

Kaye was wide awake and tense now. "Who was that?" she asked as soon as he hung up.

"Johnny Hrljic." Jake was up and pulling clothes out of his drawers. He left the room for a moment and returned with a small cassette recorder.

"Help me set this up, would you? This is bigger than the one I use in the courtroom, and I'll need help getting it secure."

Kaye's tension was replaced by a chill of fear as she sat up on the edge of the bed. "You're going out?"

He didn't look up at her. "I have to, honey." He went into the bathroom and came back with a roll of adhesive tape.

Kaye stared at him, unable to move. "Where are you going?"

"Johnny Hrljic wants to meet with me."

"It's the middle of the night!"

He sounded faintly amused. "Not exactly, but I guess he just heard some new rumors that have him scared. He wants to see what *I've* heard and find out if I have any idea who the moles might be." He looked up at her and grinned.

She did not smile back. It sounded dangerous. "You might get hurt." She was trying hard not to tremble.

"I might also clear Bill's name. Help a lot of innocent people. I might actually be finished with this whole mess." He worked with the equipment and wires. "Come on, honey. I need your help with this."

She got to her feet and hesitantly picked up the small microphone. "Shouldn't you call for someone to go with you? A backup or something?"

"I don't have time. If I'm not there within an hour, my little bird may fly." He handed her the role of tape. "Besides, I'm fairly certain our phone is tapped."

Kaye gasped in astonishment. He had mentioned the possibility before, but never with such certainty.

He didn't look at her as he went on. "Here, put the mike right up against my sternum. Then wrap the tape all the way around my chest. I'll wear my black boots. The recorder can go inside one of them."

She did as she was told, though her fingers were clumsy with nervousness. Going out at night alone to meet Hrljic seemed like a foolhardy thing to do. Didn't Jake have any sense left to see that himself? But she kept her thoughts to herself as she wrapped the tape around his chest, securing the microphone in place.

"This is really going to hurt when we pull the tape off," she said, looking at the hair on his back. Her voice sounded close to tears.

Jake laughed mirthlessly. "It would hurt a lot more if the microphone fell and Johnny noticed it."

Honorable Intentions 155

Kaye forced herself to smile slightly even though she suddenly found it hard to breathe. She concentrated on taping the wire that ran down his stomach and along the inside of his right leg. Then Jake put on a bulky flannel shirt and pants that were cut rather full. He plugged the microphone wire into the recorder and slipped that into the top of his boot.

"How do I look?" He turned around slowly, giving her a chance to survey him carefully. "Any sign of anything?"

She shook her head. He was a big man, but usually looked fairly trim. Tonight he looked bulky, just as he wanted to. "You look fine."

Jake nodded, then went over to his nightstand. He wrote on a small piece of paper and came over to her.

"If I'm not back by eight, call this number and ask for Brad Howard. Tell him that I went to meet Johnny Hrljic at this address." Kaye saw that the address was in the old warehouse district on the city's west side. She nodded slowly.

She followed him out to the foyer and watched while he put on his heavy sheepskin jacket. She was so afraid for him, but didn't know what to say. If she only could talk him out of the whole thing she would, but she knew Jake. He would be determined to see this thing through to the end.

"Well, see you later, kid," he said with a bravado that rang hollow in her ears. "Don't stay up. You can get six or seven hours of sleep." He gave her a quick kiss, then went to the door.

As he opened it, he glanced back at her. She flew into his arms and clung to him for a brief moment, all her fear and love warring within her. She was so afraid that she might never see him again, yet she loved him with all her being, and couldn't stop him from doing something he thought he should.

"Please, be careful," she whispered.

"Hey, don't worry about me. Worry about getting your beauty sleep." He hugged her tightly to him, and she felt the microphone pressing against her.

"Jake, I love you." There were tears in her eyes, and her voice quivered.

"I'll be fine, honey. Really, I will." He gave her another quick hug, then released her. Abruptly, he was gone.

Kaye stood alone in the cold entryway, feeling frightened. Her mouth was dry, and her hands were clammy. "Jake, please come back to me," she whispered to the closed door. But only silence answered her.

She went back to the bedroom and placed Jake's note on her nightstand. Then she turned off the light and pulled the covers tightly around her. She felt cold—oh, so cold. She was shivering; then she was crying.

"Jake, come home soon," she whispered to the darkness.

11

KAYE NEVER EXPECTED to get back to sleep. She lay awake for hours watching the red numbers on her digital alarm clock change. Where was Jake? Was he safe? Why had she let him go?

The cats came and cuddled up close to her legs, but she was too restless to lie still. Eventually, they stomped over to Jake's pillow and curled up there. She turned over to stare at the clock again.

Sometime after four, she must have dozed off, for the ringing of the phone startled her. She jumped up, her heart pounding as she stared for a long moment toward the sound. She was almost afraid to answer, but finally she snatched up the receiver.

"Kaye?"

"Jake?" Relief came flooding through her. "Are you all right?"

"Kaye, listen to me." His voice was firm and authoritative and brought her quickly to attention.

"You still have that number that I gave you before I left?"

"Yes," she said, slightly puzzled.

"Okay. I have to go away for a few days. If you need to get hold of me for any reason, call that number."

Kaye put her hand to her head. What was going on? Why did he have to go away? A tremor of fear began to grow. Something was wrong.

"Jake? What's the matter?"

"Nothing, honey. Everything's fine. Really."

Something in his voice reassured her, and she gripped the phone a little less tightly. "But why do you have to go away? Where are you going?"

He didn't answer. She heard a murmur of voices in the background; then Jake was back. "Kaye, they don't want you to use our phone unless you absolutely have to."

She remembered his fear last night that the phone was tapped.

"At ten this morning, please call that number I gave you. Okay?"

"Yes," she said.

"I love you, honey. See you soon."

The line went dead before she had time to reply. "Jake?" she called, then stopped, feeling unhappy. She had let him go without saying anything. She didn't even know how long he would be away.

Honorable Intentions 159

She put the receiver down slowly. He sounded fine. Maybe this was the end, and their lives would actually go back to normal. She smiled a little at the thought. She wasn't sure what normal was anymore.

It was just five o'clock, not much time left for a good night's sleep, but Kaye curled up under the covers anyway and slept soundly for an hour or so. Then she showered and got dressed. The house seemed so quiet that it was unnerving. She made herself some coffee, but it tasted bitter. The emptiness of the house was getting to her, reminding her of all her unanswered questions. She poured the coffee down the drain. She'd go out for breakfast. It was time to start getting out among people for a change.

She put on her hat and coat and left the building. A dark brown car was just turning onto their street. It pulled up next to her.

"Mrs. Corrigan?"

Before Kaye even had time to feel frightened, the woman in the passenger side of the car was showing Kaye her badge. She was a policewoman. A plainclothes detective.

"Are you Mrs. Corrigan?" the woman repeated.

"Yes, I am," Kaye breathed. She felt slightly concerned, but the other woman was smiling at her.

"We have orders to keep an eye on your home and give you a lift to work."

Kaye blinked in surprise, a shiver running down her spine. She had police protection? Protection from what? Flustered, she didn't know what to say. "Oh, thank you."

"Are you going to work now?"

"No." Kaye shook her head. "No, I'm going to breakfast."

The woman glanced at her male partner. He shrugged slightly. "We've got orders to keep an eye on you," the woman said compassionately.

"Sure, okay." Kaye laughed. She had decided she didn't want to be alone, but she hadn't thought she'd find company this fast.

The man got out and opened the back door of the car for Kaye. "We don't lose too many fares," he joked as Kaye noticed there were no handles on the inside of the doors.

They went to a twenty-four-hour restaurant just a few blocks from her home. The food was adequate and the service fast. Before long, they had their breakfast in front of them.

The patrolman's name was Gus. He was a stolid white man in his forties who ate his meal quickly and dispassionately. The only thing Kaye gleaned from his conversation was that he'd been a policeman for almost fifteen years.

Chita was easier to talk to. She was black and in her late twenties, with the slender build and high cheekbones of a model. She had a teacher husband and twin girls two years old. Her father and an uncle had been policemen before her.

The time passed pleasantly. "It'll be my treat," Kaye insisted when they were done.

Gus laughed. "The restaurants usually just take care of it."

"This time they won't." Kaye picked up the check and carried it to the cashier. She wasn't going to be near anything resembling a payoff ever again.

When they dropped her off at work, Chita handed Kaye a business card. "Give us a call when you're ready to go home. That's the number for our duty officer. They all know about you. Your escort has been requested from pretty high up."

Kaye was puzzled by all the attention, but thanked them. Surely if she was getting such protection, then so was Jake. He must be all right.

"Yes, I know that he's not in court," Kaye sighed into the phone.

The reporter was insistent. "Do you know where he is right now, Mrs. Corrigan?"

"He's away on personal business." She was getting better at handling the press. She didn't know where Jake was, but she did know enough not to admit that.

"Do you know when Judge Corrigan will return?"

"When his business is finished," she replied evenly, and hung up.

And she didn't know when that would be. She had talked to Brad Howard at the number Jake had given her, but he wouldn't tell her where Jake was. All Brad could say was that Jake was staying out of town for a few days because of some work he was doing. He assured her that Jake was well and would be home in a couple of days. Not much information to ease her battered nerves.

She kept going over her brief conversation with Jake, trying to remember just how he sounded. Surely, if something was wrong, she'd know it. She just wished she didn't feel so alone. She noticed that her other two telephone lines were flashing. There was no way she'd get any work done with all these interruptions.

She instructed the main switchboard to take messages instead of putting the calls through to her department, then packed up her papers and went up to the executive office suite. The conference room she had used before was occupied, so she would use the district manager's office for the day.

She settled herself in and gazed about, mildly interested. Less than two months ago, she would have memorized every detail of the sumptuous office toward the day when she would have one just like it. But she was no longer certain that was what she wanted. Actually, she wasn't sure just what she did want.

Things that had seemed absolutely necessary before, like that association presidency, were lost and only slightly missed. Jake and his love were all that really mattered. All she wanted the future to hold. The thought of children came to her mind again, and it was a pleasant thought. A part of her and Jake to carry on.

Unfortunately, however nice those thoughts were, they were not helping her get her work done. She resolutely put the fantasies out of her mind and concentrated on the papers in front of her. She had her weekly sales reports to prepare. That was what she was paid for. If she wanted to daydream, she should do it on her own time.

Kaye worked through to the early afternoon, then took a lunch break. With her shoes off and her feet resting on a lower drawer, she ate her bacon, lettuce,

Honorable Intentions 163

and tomato sandwich. The windows of this office looked down the river and out onto the lake. It was a lovely wintery view, and Kaye feasted her eyes on it as she satisfied her stomach's cravings.

"Oh, Kaye. We've been looking all over for you."

Startled, Kaye looked up into her assistant's anxious face. Her first thought was that something had happened to Jake. "Why? What's the matter?"

"You have a bunch of messages at the switchboard. They're marked urgent."

"Reporters?" Kaye asked suspiciously.

"No, I think they're from your relatives. I mean, your in-laws."

Kaye slipped her shoes on quickly, panic racing through her blood. Something had happened to Jake. She knew it.

She raced down the hall to the central switchboard. It was on the same floor as the executive offices, but they might have been in different towns for all anybody thought to look there for her. She went quickly through her messages. Most were from reporters, but three were from Danny and one from Marcia. They all left the same message: a doctor's name and telephone number.

She hurried back to her temporary office, her heart filled with foreboding.

She quickly dialed the number she had been given and reached a Dr. Merkel's office. He was at the hospital and not available to speak to her.

"Would you like to leave a message?" the receptionist asked.

Kaye clenched her teeth in frustration. She supposed that was what she'd have to do. "Yes, please. This is Kaye Corrigan—"

"Oh, Mrs. Corrigan," the woman broke in, sounding almost pleasant. "We've been trying to reach you. Your husband's mother has been taken to St. Mary's Medical Center."

Kaye was stunned. "What happened to her?"

"I'm sorry." The cold, impersonal wall was back up. "You'll have to speak to the doctor." The line went dead.

Oh, dear Lord. This was something she had not expected. She had to reach Jake. He would want to be here. Would they let him come back?

She got her purse and found the number, but hung up before she finished dialing. What would she tell him? Maybe she'd better find out what was wrong before she talked to Jake.

Kaye put on her coat and was about to have one of the secretaries call her a cab when she stopped. Was she really in danger? Jake or someone must have thought so, or they wouldn't have arranged the police escort. She dialed the number on the card that Chita had given her that morning and was told to wait inside the office. The police officers would come for her.

She was standing at the window nervously twisting her handkerchief and chafing at the delay when she heard the soft voice behind her.

"Hi."

Kaye turned and saw Chita's smiling face.

"Since we're such close friends, we decided to take the call. Besides, Gus and I figure that we owe you

Honorable Intentions 165

at least a couple more rides for the breakfast."

Kaye just nodded.

Chita looked sharply into her face. "Something wrong, Mrs. Corrigan?"

Kaye shrugged. "I don't know. My husband's mother was taken to the hospital, and I don't know what's wrong."

"And you want to get there quick?"

Kaye nodded.

Without further words, they went down the stairs and out onto the street where Gus was waiting. Chita quickly put Kaye in the cage in back.

"Run it hot," Chita ordered Gus.

Before Chita had finished closing her own door, the police car was hurtling out into oncoming taffic, siren wailing, dome lights flashing. They made the five-mile trip through heavy traffic in less than fifteen minutes.

Kaye thanked them and hurried into the building where she was directed to the tenth floor. The nurse at that desk sent her into the waiting room. Marcia was sitting there, a worried look on her face. She got up when Kaye entered.

"Oh, I'm so glad that you could come." She looked beyond her. "Where's Jake? Danny's been trying to find him all morning."

"Jake can't be reached easily," Kaye told her. "How is his mother?"

"I don't know. Danny's with the doctors now. They think she's had a heart attack."

Marcia walked across the small room, wringing her hands. "Mike and Lucy are in Florida, of all things, but thank God Jake's around. Danny's not good in a crisis." She stopped and turned around to face Kaye. "When will Jake get here?"

"He's out of town, and I haven't tried to reach him, yet," Kaye told her. "I wanted to find out what was wrong first."

"You haven't tried to reach him?" Marcia was astonished. "Don't you think you ought to? After all, that's his mother in there, and she may be dying!"

Kaye felt her face pale as fear clutched her stomach. "She's dying?"

"Well, she may be," Marcia said, and burst into tears.

The door opened, and Danny came in with a doctor. He glanced briefly at his wife before coming over to Kaye.

"This is my sister-in-law, Kaye. Jake's wife," he told the doctor, then turned to Kaye. "This is Mom's doctor, Dr. Merkel."

"How is she, Doctor?" Kaye asked brusquely, brushing aside the usual pleasantries.

"Resting right now. We think she's had a mild heart attack, but she isn't in any real danger."

Kaye sighed in relief, but couldn't help glancing over at Marcia.

"Where's Jake?" Danny asked.

"He's out of town," Kaye began.

"And she hasn't even called him yet," Marcia added for her.

"I wanted to find out what was wrong before I did."

"Well, I'd wait a little longer," the doctor said. "I

Honorable Intentions 167

should be getting some tests results soon." He nodded to them all and left.

Kaye sat down. The almost sleepless night was catching up with her. She felt worn out and knew she was functioning on nervous energy.

"This is Jake's fault, you know," Marcia said suddenly.

Kaye looked up, but Danny spoke first.

"We don't know that," he said. "Lots of things could have brought it on."

"Like what?" Marcia snapped. "She's been worried sick over what everyone's saying about Jake."

Kaye felt sick herself. She got to her feet and wandered over to the window. When was it all going to end? she wondered as she gazed down on the parking lot. If Jake's involvement really had caused his mother's heart attack, how would he live with that knowledge? He had only been trying to do something good in clearing Bill's name, yet so many hurts had come from it.

It was time for at least some of those hurts to end, Kaye decided suddenly. Marcia and Danny were involved in an argument of their own, and she slipped out of the waiting room. Dr. Merkel was at the end of the hall, and she went to him.

"Can I see my mother-in-law?" she asked.

"She was sleeping," the doctor said. "But we can check."

He led her down the hall and stopped in front of a door. Kaye felt her stomach tighten as he pushed it open. Jake's mother was lying on the bed. Her face looked tired, but peaceful. The eyes were as bright and piercing as ever as they quickly went from the doctor to her.

"Hello, dear. Please come in."

Kaye went over and kissed her lightly on the cheek. "Hello, Mother. How are you?"

"I was a little tired, but now I'm bored and irritated. I don't like being under some one else's control."

"I don't like hospitals either."

"Only a few minutes," the doctor warned, then left them alone.

Kaye moved a chair closer to the bed and sat there in silence for a long moment. Deciding to tell Jake's mother that Jake was innocent was one thing. Doing it was another. Where did she begin?

"Where is Jake?"

"Jake?" Kaye responded, slightly flustered.

The older woman smiled and went on in a gentle voice. "Yes, Jake. You may remember him. He's your husband, my son."

Kaye felt foolish and smiled sheepishly. "I'm sorry. My mind was wandering."

"I haven't seen Jake since Thanksgiving," his mother went on. "Is he going to fit me into his schedule and pay me a visit? I'm not up to as much moving around in the winter as I used to be, or I would have tracked him down myself."

"He... Jake can't visit anyone right now."

"Can't is a rather strong word, Kaye." The blue eyes turned to stone and bored into her soul. "Why can't he? Is he in prison?"

"No," Kaye snapped. The question shocked her

out of her sidestepping, careful answers. "Of course, he isn't."

A slight smile seemed to be playing on her mother-in-law's lips. "Then where is he?"

Kaye looked for a long moment into Mrs. Corrigan's sharp blue eyes. It was time to be blunt. "He left town early this morning. My talks with him were rather guarded, but I think he's in protective custody."

"Then he's finally done with that stupid charade?"

Kaye had been prepared for questions and further explanations, but she could not speak. She just stared at her mother-in-law, robbed of her voice by the question.

"Well, you didn't think I believed all that nonsense, did you?" Mrs. Corrigan asked gently. "Though I have to admit I was getting a bit tired of it all. Don't you think he dragged the whole thing out a bit too long?"

Kaye just shook her head, not knowing what to say. All this time, Jake's mother had known. Kaye had been worrying about the effect of the scandal on her, and she had known the truth. Suddenly, Kaye found that she was crying and fumbled in her purse for a handkerchief. Jake's mother handed her a box of tissues.

"They come with the room," she explained.

Kaye nodded and wiped away her tears. "I didn't think you knew. I didn't think anybody knew."

Jake's mother smiled gently. "I didn't really know. I just believed."

Kaye blinked in confusion.

"Which was it for you, Kaye?"

She shrugged, feeling somewhat ashamed. "A little of both. I sort of forced him to tell me a month or so ago."

Mrs. Corrigan nodded and reached out to take Kaye's hand. Neither spoke for a time.

"It must have been hard for you," the older woman finally said.

Kaye shrugged. "It wasn't so bad. We had each other."

"I'm glad he told you. Jake can be so stubborn sometimes."

There was another long silence. Then Jake's mother spoke. "As long as it's time for confessions, tell me why you and Jake didn't come for Christmas dinner."

"How did you know—"

"I still go to church at St. Pat's on Christmas."

Kaye looked away, feeling ashamed. She didn't know how to reply, and blew her nose. "Reporters were following us everywhere, and we were afraid that they'd bother you too much."

"Is that what Jake decided?"

"It was sort of a family decision."

"No, it wasn't a family decision," Jake's mother said sharply. "I wasn't involved in it. I have a good idea who was behind it, though, and right now she's probably telling everyone that my heart attack was all Jake's fault."

Kaye could not hide her surprise.

"Oh, I know how Marcia is," Jake's mother assured her. "She's been trying for years to push Danny into a position of prominence and has failed. Now, all she's got left is trying to make him the favorite son.

Honorable Intentions 171

I wish she would just support him the way you support Jake. Of couse, she wouldn't. She'd run at the first hint of trouble. Jake is one lucky man, and I intend to tell him that the next time I see him." She paused. "That is, if he ever decides to come by again."

"He will," Kaye assured her.

"He may wish he hadn't before I finish with him."

Kaye laughed as she stood up. "I'd better go and call Jake. I'm sure I've been in here too long." She walked toward the door.

"Kaye," Jake's mother called.

She turned at the door.

"I'm glad Jake married you."

"Thank you," Kaye said simply, and left. She was surprised and touched and felt like singing. Once Jake was home again, everything would be perfect.

Down the hall there was a phone booth, and Kaye hurried toward it. She dialed the number Jake had given her and explained who she was to the woman who answered. She was told to hang up and remain at the phone. In less than five minutes, Jake called. She felt like crying with relief when she heard his voice. He really was all right.

"Jake?"

"Kaye, sweetheart. How are you? How is Mom?"

"She's doing well. Fine, in fact. We had a nice talk."

"Did she ask about me?"

Kaye laughed, feeling lighthearted all of a sudden. "No, she forgot all about you. Of course, she asked where you were and hoped that you were done with your 'stupid charade,' as she put it."

Jake was silent for a long time.

"How did she know?"

"She said that she didn't really know, she just believed."

This time it was Jake's turn to laugh. "She probably figured that I'd be afraid to do the things I was accused of."

Kaye giggled hysterically, like a schoolgirl. "Were you?"

"You're darn right," he replied. "My mother's tough. She never was the type to wait until Dad got home. She took care of all disciplining immediately."

They were both silent for a long moment.

"Anyway, is she really all right?"

"Yes," Kaye answered. "And she said to tell you that the publicity about you was not the cause of her heart attack."

"I wondered," he admitted.

"So did I." She paused. "Where are you, Jake?"

"I'm not sure, but don't you worry anymore. My little late-night visit got even more evidence than I'd dreamed possible, and they whisked me away so they could spring the announcement to the press as a total surprise."

"When are you coming home?"

"Sunday. We're going to play a little game of meet the press. I want you with me."

"Okay," Kaye answered, unable to keep the doubt out of her voice.

"Don't worry, Kaye. This time it'll be fun."

She couldn't see how that was possible, but she'd

believe anything, she was so happy to hear from him. "I love you."

"I love you too, honey." On that simple note, the line went dead, but the smile stayed on her lips.

12

KAYE PACED UP and down the little reception room on the second floor of the Federal Building. It was early Sunday afternoon, and she was waiting for Jake to arrive. Her stomach was dong a Mexican hat dance around her navel, telling her she should have eaten breakfast.

A plainclothes detective had brought her here about a half-hour ago, but no one had told her what time Jake would come. She had been escorted into this room to wait. Wait and pace, that is. Somehow it seemed like years since she had seen Jake.

She had felt giddy and light-headed all morning. Jake was coming home, and he was going to be cleared. Everybody would know he was innocent. She had hugged Nip and Tuck until they had both hidden from her exuberance.

Then it had taken her hours to decide on what to wear. She'd had a wild impulse to wear the blue silk dress that she had worn to that political Christmas party, along with a full complement of jewelry. Jake would have died. That thought had made her laugh so hard that tears had come to her eyes. Nip, the bolder of the cats, had peered around the corner at her for a few moments and then had dashed away.

She had finally decided on a simple gray suit. It was dignified and businesslike. Very fitting for the press conference, she had thought. Besides, the temperature was supposed to hover around zero all day. But as she waited in the Federal Building later in the day, she worried. Maybe she should have worn a dress. Maybe Jake would have—

She turned suddenly at the sound of a door opening, and all her worries about clothes vanished as Jake walked in. It was so wonderful to see him. She ran straight into his arms and lost herself completely in his bear hug. It felt so good to be back in his arms again.

He let her go, and they stood looking at each other for a long moment, as if they were hungry just for the sight of each other. Kaye felt strangely tongue-tied.

"Are you all right?" he asked.

She nodded. "How about you?"

It was his turn to nod. "It would have been a better vacation if you'd been along."

She smiled and squeezed his hand. "Your mom's doing real well."

"I'm glad."

Honorable Intentions

The U.S. attorney came into the room and called Jake over for a briefing. Kaye pretended to glance about the room, but her eyes always came back to Jake. Why had they had such a trivial conversation? They had done better on their first date.

Maybe it was because their emotions were running so high now. She had been so worried about Jake, and then so relieved to see him that mere words seemed banal. She wanted to hold him, to feel him lying next to her, to experience the power of his love. But first there were formalities to go through...

"We're just about ready to start, Mrs. Corrigan."

Kaye turned around as an FBI agent spoke to her. Jake came over to take her arm, and they all went into a large conference room. They walked onto a stage where the governor was talking to Brad Howard. The press was filing into the rows of folding chairs below them.

Twenty minutes later, Kaye stood next to Jake and listened to the United States Attorney explain the undercover operation and tell about the judges and lawyers who had helped them collect evidence.

"Without them, we would never have been able to gather the evidence we have," the attorney said. "Over the next few months a grand jury will review the testimony and issue indictments. From what I have heard of the evidence, few levels of our court system will remain untouched." He turned and waved Jake forward.

"I'd like to give special praise to one person in particular. Or maybe I should say one family."

The attorney put his hand on Jake's shoulder. "Judge

John Corrigan here was one of our best sources of evidence over the past two years. Before that time, his brother Bill, also a housing court judge, helped us considerably. When he was killed in an unfortunate accident, Jake willingly stepped forward to take Bill's place. I think I can safely say that with the information gathered by just these two brothers, the courts in the city of Chicago will be much closer to providing justice for all."

He stepped back to let Jake answer questions from the press. Kaye was astonished when they even wanted to talk to her.

"Mrs. Corrigan, how long have you known about your husband's activities?"

Kaye blinked rapidly. The question jerked her out of her pleasant daydreaming. How long? She glanced at Jake. She wasn't supposed to have known at all.

"Only a short while," Kaye said.

Jake smiled at her, and Kaye could read the approval in his eyes. He had been right; talking to the press wasn't so bad this time.

"Weren't you concerned when the negative publicity began, Mrs. Corrigan?"

Jake's gaze seemed to caress her, giving her confidence and strength. She smiled at him and then at the reporter. "I had faith in Jake. Without faith, you have no marriage."

"Was it worth it, Mrs. Corrigan?"

That one was easy to answer. "It was something Jake felt that he had to do. Conscience has no cost."

"Judge, do you plan to stay on the bench?"

Honorable Intentions

"I'm going to devote my full energies to the conclusion of the investigation for the next several months."

"Then you're resigning your position in the county court system?"

"Yes."

"There are rumors that you'll be offered a position as a federal judge. Would you care to comment on that?"

Kaye looked up in surprise at Jake. A federal judgeship?

"I'm sure there will be several such rumors in the next few months," Jake said. "After I have fulfilled my obligation to the investigation, I'm going to look at a number of opportunities."

There were more questions about the investigation itself, but they were answered by the U.S. attorney, and then the governor made a short speech praising everyone. Finally, it was over, and Kaye and Jake were free to go. Someone went off to find an agent to drive them home, and they were alone in the reception room again.

Now that it was over, Kaye felt the tears start. Jake took her into his arms and held her close. It was like being in heaven to hear his heart beat against her and smell his after shave.

"Where were you?" she asked after a moment.

"At a Holiday Inn in Waterloo, Iowa."

"Sounds exciting," she said brokenly.

"It was."

"Why did I have police protection?" she asked after a moment.

"I insisted on it."

"But why?"

He looked out the window and seemed reluctant to answer. "I was afraid Hrljic might try something."

"Against me?" Kaye was floored.

"That would be a good way of getting back at me if he suspected the truth," Jake pointed out, then tightened his arms around her. "This conference will end that, though. Now that the word is out on the investigation, they'll all be rushing around trying to protect their own skins." He kissed her again, hungrily and long.

There was a loud clearing of a throat behind them, and, startled, they looked around.

"Need a ride home, folks?"

"We'd appreciate it," Jake replied.

"No," Kaye interrupted. "We have to go to St. Mary's Medical Center first."

Jake looked at her.

"You're in enough trouble with your mother already," Kaye said. "You'd better not fool around anymore."

"Well, what do you think?" Jake asked her.

Kaye snuggled up even closer under the covers. "I don't think I want to eat badly enough to get up."

"We could eat in here."

"I've heard of breakfast in bed, but *dinner* in bed?"

"Why not?" He laughed.

"Because there are other things I'd rather do." She slid her hands over his rough chest, marveling at the surge of desire that raced through her as she touched him.

Their bed had seemed so empty these last few days. She had missed their lovemaking, certainly, but she had also missed just having him near her as she slept. It had been awful to wake up in the middle of the night and know she was alone. The room had seemed colder than usual, and too quiet. Without the sound of his breathing, it had taken her hours to go to sleep. She hoped they would never be apart again. She wrapped her arms around his body and laid her head on his chest.

"We've been apart before," she mused. "Why were these last few days so terrible? Worse than ever before?"

"I know I was worried as hell about you," Jake admitted. His hands roamed over her back, touching her in a possessive way that made her move even closer to him. "That doesn't make for a good night's sleep."

"You know, you never told me what you did with all those bribes you were pretending to take," she pointed out. "Are you going to have to give anything back?"

"Like what?"

"Like my necklace."

Jake laughed, and she felt the rumbling deep inside him. It was a comforting feeling. "I told you I bought that with my own money. Don't you believe me when I tell you something?"

She didn't say anything for a time, just idly moved

her hand across his skin, enjoying the feel of the muscles and the sound of his heart beating beneath her ear. "Not always," she said with a laugh. "So where's the bribe money?"

"In a special account. I never used any of it, so you don't have to worry."

The room was dark, and she could not see his expression. "Was it worth it?"

He was silent for a long time. "Yes, I think so," he finally said. "But that's something you'll have to answer for yourself. You paid a price for my involvement, too. Was the price too high?"

His arms moved to hold her closer, and she lay half on his body. "Sometimes, I thought it was," she admitted. "Like when I had to resign as nominee for president of the merchants' association. But then, after a while, I began to wonder if that's what I really wanted. I began to think that my family was more important than any career advancement."

"What if they offer the presidency to you again, now that I'm cleared?" Jake asked.

"I don't know," she said. "I really don't know. Part of me still wants it, just to prove that I could do it if I had the chance. But part of me wants to throw it back in their faces."

"Does that add up to all of you?"

"No." She laughed and tickled him quickly. "The other part of me thinks maybe there's more to life than a successful career and that I should take advantage of the free time I'm being offered."

"To keep your husband happy?" he asked, his hands suddenly becoming more insistent.

"Actually, I've been thinking about children," she admitted. His caress stopped, and she raised herself up on her elbow to look into his face. "What's wrong? Don't you want kids?"

"Of course I do," he said quietly. "I'd love a family. The very idea of having kids with you lights me up like a Christmas tree, but are you sure it's what you want? You've been pretty devoted to your career up to now."

"My priorities have changed over the past few months," she said.

He rolled her over onto her back so that he was above her, and planted tiny, whispery kisses along the base of her neck. "So how soon were you thinking of starting this family?"

She laughed. "I think we need at least nine months."

"We probably ought to start practicing right away. I want to be sure I do it right." His kisses were growing deeper as his lips slowly brushed her skin.

She sighed and turned her head in response to his movements. A sweet languidness was melting her bones, robbing her of all thought. His hands were on her waist, sliding upward to her breasts. His rougher skin left hers tingling, aching for more than his caress.

His lips moved down to her breasts, capturing each rosy peak and tugging at it slightly. Her longing grew, and her body arched against his, her breath quickening as her lips sought his. His mouth returned to hers, drinking deeply of her warmth and love, and silently promising her all she wanted.

Their lovemaking was a mixture of tenderness and reckless passion as they brought each other up to the crest of love and on through a cascading explosion of stars.

"Jake," she murmured much later as she lay in the security of his embrace.

"Hmm?"

"I love you."

"And I love you, Kaye."

"I always knew your intentions were honorable," she said drowsily.

"You kept the faith."

His kiss awoke the fires once more, and she gave herself to him in blissful adandon.

WONDERFUL ROMANCE NEWS:

Do you know about the exciting SECOND CHANCE AT LOVE/TO HAVE AND TO HOLD newsletter? Are you on our *free* mailing list? If reading all about your favorite authors, getting sneak previews of their latest releases, and being filled in on all the latest happenings and events in the romance world sounds good to you, then you'll love our SECOND CHANCE AT LOVE and TO HAVE AND TO HOLD Romance News.

If you'd like to be added to our mailing list, just fill out the coupon below and send it in...and we'll send you your *free* newsletter every three months — hot off the press.

☐ *Yes, I would like to receive your free SECOND CHANCE AT LOVE/TO HAVE AND TO HOLD newsletter.*

Name _____
Address _____
City _____ **State/Zip** _____

Please return this coupon to:
   Berkley Publishing
   200 Madison Avenue, New York, New York 10016
   Att: Irene Majuk

HERE'S WHAT READERS ARE SAYING ABOUT

To Have and to Hold

"Your TO HAVE AND TO HOLD series is a fabulous and long overdue idea."
—*A. D., Upper Darby, PA**

"I have been reading romance novels for over ten years and feel the TO HAVE AND TO HOLD series is the best I have read. It's exciting, sensitive, refreshing, well written. Many thanks for a series of books I can relate to."
—*O. K., Bensalem, PA**

"I enjoy your books tremendously."
—*J. C., Houston, TX**

"I love the books and read them over and over."
—*E. K., Warren, MI**

"You have another winner with the new TO HAVE AND TO HOLD series."
—*R. P., Lincoln Park, MI**

"I love the new series TO HAVE AND TO HOLD."
—*M. L., Cleveland, OH**

"I've never written a fan letter before, but TO HAVE AND TO HOLD is fantastic."
—*E. S., Narberth, PA**

*Name and address available upon request

Second Chance at Love

- ___ 07246-X **SEASON OF MARRIAGE #158** Diane Crawford
- ___ 07576-0 **EARTHLY SPLENDOR #161** Sharon Francis
- ___ 07580-9 **STARRY EYED #165** Maureen Norris
- ___ 07592-2 **SPARRING PARTNERS #177** Lauren Fox
- ___ 07593-0 **WINTER WILDFIRE #178** Elissa Curry
- ___ 07594-9 **AFTER THE RAIN #179** Aimée Duvall
- ___ 07595-7 **RECKLESS DESIRE #180** Nicola Andrews
- ___ 07596-5 **THE RUSHING TIDE #181** Laura Eaton
- ___ 07597-3 **SWEET TRESPASS #182** Diana Mars
- ___ 07598-1 **TORRID NIGHTS #183** Beth Brookes
- ___ 07800-X **WINTERGREEN #184** Jeanne Grant
- ___ 07801-8 **NO EASY SURRENDER #185** Jan Mathews
- ___ 07802-6 **IRRESISTIBLE YOU #186** Claudia Bishop
- ___ 07803-4 **SURPRISED BY LOVE #187** Jasmine Craig
- ___ 07804-2 **FLIGHTS OF FANCY #188** Linda Barlow
- ___ 07805-0 **STARFIRE #189** Lee Williams
- ___ 07806-9 **MOONLIGHT RHAPSODY #190** Kay Robbins
- ___ 07807-7 **SPELLBOUND #191** Kate Nevins
- ___ 07808-5 **LOVE THY NEIGHBOR #192** Frances Davies
- ___ 07809-3 **LADY WITH A PAST #193** Elissa Curry
- ___ 07810-7 **TOUCHED BY LIGHTNING #194** Helen Carter
- ___ 07811-5 **NIGHT FLAME #195** Sarah Crewe
- ___ 07812-3 **SOMETIMES A LADY #196** Jocelyn Day
- ___ 07813-1 **COUNTRY PLEASURES #197** Lauren Fox
- ___ 07814-X **TOO CLOSE FOR COMFORT #198** Liz Grady
- ___ 07815-8 **KISSES INCOGNITO #199** Christa Merlin
- ___ 07816-6 **HEAD OVER HEELS #200** Nicola Andrews
- ___ 07817-4 **BRIEF ENCHANTMENT #201** Susanna Collins
- ___ 07818-2 **INTO THE WHIRLWIND #202** Laurel Blake
- ___ 07819-0 **HEAVEN ON EARTH #203** Mary Haskell
- ___ 07820-4 **BELOVED ADVERSARY #204** Thea Frederick
- ___ 07821-2 **SEASWEPT #205** Maureen Norris
- ___ 07822-0 **WANTON WAYS #206** Katherine Granger
- ___ 07823-9 **A TEMPTING MAGIC #207** Judith Yates

All of the above titles are $1.95
Prices may be slightly higher in Canada.

Available at your local bookstore or return this form to:

SECOND CHANCE AT LOVE
Book Mailing Service
P.O. Box 690, Rockville Centre, NY 11571

Please send me the titles checked above. I enclose _____. Include 75¢ for postage and handling if one book is ordered; 25¢ per book for two or more not to exceed $1.75. California, Illinois, New York and Tennessee residents please add sales tax.

NAME _____

ADDRESS _____

CITY _____ STATE/ZIP _____

(allow six weeks for delivery)   SK-41b

NEW FROM THE PUBLISHERS OF *SECOND CHANCE AT LOVE!*

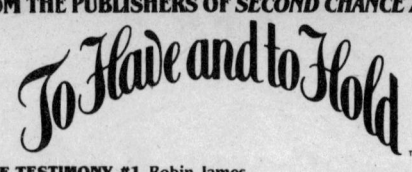

To Have and to Hold

___	THE TESTIMONY #1 Robin James	06928-0
___	A TASTE OF HEAVEN #2 Jennifer Rose	06929-9
___	TREAD SOFTLY #3 Ann Cristy	06930-2
___	THEY SAID IT WOULDN'T LAST #4 Elaine Tucker	06931-0
___	GILDED SPRING #5 Jenny Bates	06932-9
___	LEGAL AND TENDER #6 Candice Adams	06933-7
___	THE FAMILY PLAN #7 Nuria Wood	06934-5
___	HOLD FAST 'TIL DAWN #8 Mary Haskell	06935-3
___	HEART FULL OF RAINBOWS #9 Melanie Randolph	06936-1
___	I KNOW MY LOVE #10 Vivian Connolly	06937-X
___	KEYS TO THE HEART #11 Jennifer Rose	06938-8
___	STRANGE BEDFELLOWS #12 Elaine Tucker	06939-6
___	MOMENTS TO SHARE #13 Katherine Granger	06940-X
___	SUNBURST #14 Jeanne Grant	06941-8
___	WHATEVER IT TAKES #15 Cally Hughes	06942-6
___	LADY LAUGHING EYES #16 Lee Damon	06943-4
___	ALL THAT GLITTERS #17 Mary Haskell	06944-2
___	PLAYING FOR KEEPS #18 Elissa Curry	06945-0
___	PASSION'S GLOW #19 Marilyn Brian	06946-9
___	BETWEEN THE SHEETS #20 Tricia Adams	06947-7
___	MOONLIGHT AND MAGNOLIAS #21 Vivian Connolly	06948-5
___	A DELICATE BALANCE #22 Kate Wellington	06949-3
___	KISS ME, CAIT #23 Elissa Curry	07825-5
___	HOMECOMING #24 Ann Cristy	07826-3
___	TREASURE TO SHARE #25 Cally Hughes	07827-1
___	THAT CHAMPAGNE FEELING #26 Claudia Bishop	07828-X
___	KISSES SWEETER THAN WINE #27 Jennifer Rose	07829-8
___	TROUBLE IN PARADISE #28 Jeanne Grant	07830-1
___	HONORABLE INTENTIONS #29 Adrienne Edwards	07831-X
___	PROMISES TO KEEP #30 Vivian Connolly	07832-8
___	CONFIDENTIALLY YOURS #31 Petra Diamond	07833-6

All Titles are $1.95

Prices may be slightly higher in Canada.

Available at your local bookstore or return this form to:

SECOND CHANCE AT LOVE
Book Mailing Service
P.O. Box 690, Rockville Centre, NY 11571

Please send me the titles checked above. I enclose _____. Include 75¢ for postage and handling if one book is ordered; 25¢ per book for two or more not to exceed $1.75. California, Illinois, New York and Tennessee residents please add sales tax.

NAME _____

ADDRESS _____

CITY _____ STATE/ZIP _____

(allow six weeks for delivery)

THTH #67